THE SPREAD

BOOK 3 (THE STAND)

IAIN ROB WRIGHT

ULCERATED PRESS

Don't miss out on your FREE Iain Rob Wright horror pack. Five terrifying books sent straight to your inbox.

No strings attached & signing up is a doddle.

For more information just visit the back of this book.

S amantha Vickers, Choirikell's sole childminder, was not a brave woman. She had never been in a fight, couldn't abide the tamest of rollercoasters, and driving above the speed limit sent her pulse racing. No, she was not a brave woman. Not even close. Which was why her current predicament was less than ideal.

Choirikell was under attack, which of course made no sense. The village was little more than a pinprick on the map – a few hundred people, a pub, and a whole lot of hills. Yet, attacked it had most certainly been, and not-brave Samantha Vickers found herself right in the middle of a war zone.

It had all begun on Saturday morning when Mrs Meadows cried out for help from the road outside. At first, Samantha had been reluctant to act – deciding it wasn't her business to get involved in whatever was going on – but then little Matthew Meadows had started screaming as well. The boy's desperate cries for help forced her into action, and she had unbolted her front door and rushed out into the road. There, she found a scene both confusing and bizarre.

Mrs Meadows lay on the ground with her hands up in front of her face. Grey-haired Ted Abernathy from two doors down was slapping at her with both hands – almost whipping her. He appeared drunk – possibly delirious – but that didn't excuse the blood on Mrs Meadow's face. He had lost control. Four-year-old Matthew was screeching at him to stop hurting his mammy, but he wouldn't listen. Tammy Walker and Zoe Peterson were trembling beside the hysterical boy, tears streaming down their chubby cheeks. Seeing the three terrified children forced Samantha to get involved.

What am I doing? she had asked herself as her body moved out of instinct rather than reason, but no answer came. She scooped up the children and then took a step to help Mrs Meadows, but Ted turned and whipped his arms at her, forcing her to hop out of the way.

"Take them!" Mrs Meadows cried at her through gritted, bloodstained teeth. "Sam, take them and call the pol—"

A vicious slap across the face cut the woman off. Blood gushed from her forehead, and she rolled into the foetal position, screaming. Samantha knew a hero would have stayed to help, but she had already pushed herself to the limit just by gathering the children. She needed to get them inside where it was safe. There, she could call the police and have Ted arrested. Mrs Meadows would be okay. Somebody would hear her cries and come to help. Maybe Cameron Pollock or Dale Finley. They were big, tough men. They could handle meek old Ted Abernathy.

He's a postman, for God's sake. Why's he acting like a maniac?

Samantha ushered the children into her greystone cottage and locked the front door. The night had been chilly, so the windows were already closed and secure. She did her best to calm their screaming and then lunged for the phone on the kitchen wall, immediately dialling nine–nine–nine. At first, she thought someone answered, but all she heard were garbled noises. "Hello? Hello? Hello?" She yelled again and again into the receiver, begging for help, but no one replied. She was forced to hang up, and an immediate redial gave her nothing but a rapid and continuous *tick-tick-tick* sound. In case anyone was listening, she stated, as calmly as she could, her name and address, then reiterated her need for help. Finally, she grabbed her mobile phone from the armrest of the sofa in the living room, but she couldn't get any reception at all. The signal was usually spotty up in the hills, but there was usually enough to make a call.

She was completely cut off. Alone.

What is happening?

By now, the children were getting worked up again, making sounds so pitiful that they threatened to break Samantha's heart. She glanced out of the kitchen window to reassess the situation, but Ted and Mrs Meadows had gone. The road was empty.

Maybe Mrs Meadows managed to make a run for it.

Ted is going to end up in a whole heap of trouble for this.

That's for him *to worry about. I have a job to do.*

Samantha turned and studied the terror-stricken children. They were huddled together like a batch of newborn kittens. They knew each other well, their parents taking turns to bring them to Samantha's home each morning for day care. Today had clearly been Mrs Meadow's turn. Whether Samantha liked it or not, her Saturday morning playgroup was now in session.

That was how things had started.

Now it was Tuesday afternoon and the children's parents still hadn't come to collect them. The electric was off and the road outside was chock-a-block with people she knew from the village – except they were different now.

Over the course of the weekend she had witnessed countless more horrific acts of violence, just like the one perpetrated against Mrs Meadows. What made things even more disturbing was that they all involved people she knew – her friends and neighbours. Everyone was behaving like maniacs, gradually transforming into things unrecognisable. Even now, as Samantha watched from her spare bedroom window, their bizarrely elongated limbs and soulless expressions appalled her. Great shocks of green fuzz grew all over their flesh, making them look more alien than human. Nothing at all like the people she had lived alongside for years. She even spotted Mrs Meadows. A monster now, just like all the others.

How on earth do I break it to Matthew that his mammy is...?

What? What exactly is she? Sick? Dead? Undead?

Am I dead? Is this Hell?

The three children in Samantha's care were currently napping. Tammy was nearly five, so she didn't really need a daytime sleep, but Matthew and Zoe were younger and still needed the rest. Fortunately, they all lacked the maturity to fully comprehend what was happening. While they constantly asked for their mammies and daddies, they were mostly content to play and eat snacks.

But those snacks would eventually run out, and the toys had already lost their ability to entertain. More and more, Samantha felt trapped inside her own home. She couldn't call for help, couldn't leave, and three children were relying on her to keep them safe.

How much longer can we stay here?

Until we run out of food?

Most of it in the freezer has already spoiled.

Occasionally, Samantha imagined she heard distant gunfire, but it was nothing she could be sure of. It might have been fireworks or a car backfiring. Or, as was her biggest hope, it could have been Mr McGregor somewhere, letting off his shotgun. The old fox was a tough biscuit, and he might just show up to save the day. She held on to that possibility.

The children would awaken soon. Samantha would need to have their lunch ready or they'd become unruly. Matthew, in particular, had been a handful these past few days. Did the boy instinctively know something had happened to his mother?

I'll have to use the last of the bread before it goes stale. The cheese slices are borderline too.

Samantha moved to exit the spare bedroom where the children slept together in a double bed. As she passed, Tammy slid an arm out from beneath the covers and grabbed her. The four-year-old was awake, peering up at Samantha conspiratorially. "Are they still out there?" she whispered.

Samantha frowned, keeping her own voice to a whisper. "Is *who* still out there?"

"The monsters."

Her first instinct was to scoff, but the child deserved better than that. Tammy was a good girl. Bright. "You've seen them outside?"

The little girl nodded. While most four-year-olds struggled to understand the concept of speaking quietly, Tammy always made a good job of it. "I looked out of the window while you were sleeping this morning. I seen Matthew's mammy. She looked poorly."

"I think a lot of people in the village are very sick, pet."

"Will *we* get sick?"

"No. We're safe and sound here. This will all be over soon, okay?"

Tammy nodded but seemed unconvinced. "Can I come downstairs?"

"Of course. Come on." Samantha offered a hand to help the child slip silently from beneath the thick duvet. The two of them crept downstairs into the gloomy hallway. Curtains were drawn over every window. The lights had been off since Ted had attacked Mrs Meadows.

I'm completely alone.

No. I have the children.

This isn't the end. I can't let it be.

"Can I have more cereal?" Tammy asked gently as they headed into the small lounge.

"I'm afraid we ate the last of it this morning, sweetheart. It'll have to be toast."

"Okay."

"Think I might have some chocolate spread in the cupboard, though. Keep it a secret and you can have some."

Tammy smiled. Samantha told her to go and sit in the conservatory that she'd had built to provide extra space for her daycare business. The money to do so had been left to her by a late aunt she had barely known. The conservatory was her favourite part of the house, stacked with toys, children's books, board games, and colouring pencils. It was safe, innocent. Detached from the harsh realities of the world. Dean couldn't get to her there. He couldn't break her smile. Even the pain in her twice-broken wrist went away whenever she played with the children in the bright, sunlit room. She was no longer a victim, but a protector. People trusted her to keep their children safe.

And that's what I'm going do. No matter what.

Matthew and Zoe woke up ten minutes later, and they all sat together in the conservatory, quietly eating. Without Peppa Pig dancing on the room's small television screen, things were unexpectedly lonely. TV's absence had left an unexpectedly large hole in their routine, and the silence was somehow deafening. Whiffs of cold baked bean juice and hardening bread now provided the background to their lives.

After lunch ended, Samantha's stomach continued to rumble. She had been eating less and less as the days went by, painfully aware of the increasing bareness of her cupboards. Three growing children could eat a surprising amount, and nightmares of watching them starve plagued her sleep. What if no one ever came to their rescue? What chance did they have outside among the monsters?

All the children can do is run. Are they fast enough to get away?

The thought of leaving home terrified Samantha. The thought of leaving Choirikell, even more. The dreary village had kept her safe these last three years; had kept her past at bay and allowed her to finally discover herself after thirty-seven years of self-estrangement. Her neighbours liked her – and *trusted* her – and nobody ever told her what to do. No one ever beat her for disobeying. This was the first place to ever truly become a home. A place where Dean would never hurt her ever again.

But now her neighbours were monsters and her sanctuary

was a prison. Her new-found life revealed itself to be an illusion and she found herself no stronger than before.

No. I left Dean. I packed my bags and disappeared; to start a new life from nothing. I did that. Me.

I was strong.

But if I'd been truly brave, I would've pressed charges to warn other women what he was like. I told myself I was standing up for myself, but really I was running away. I'm not brave. I've never been brave.

I can't keep these children safe.

As usual, the children brought her back from the spiralling dread inside her own mind.

"... thing's happening in the garden."

It was Tammy speaking, clearly alarmed by something. Samantha swivelled her neck so fast that it hurt. The garden fence had tilted, a weight bearing down on it from the other side. She sprung to her feet, knocking over her chair. "No," she said. "No, we've been quiet. We've been careful. How did they know we're in here?"

"It was me," said Tammy meekly. The child's hand was inside a packet of crisps, frozen mid-snatch. "When I looked out the window they saw me. I didn't want to tell you and make you mad. I-I'm sorry."

Samantha put an arm around the trembling girl and squeezed. "Don't you apologise, sweetheart, do you hear me? You've done nothing wrong. Nowt!"

Tammy started to cry, but Zoe and Matthew didn't understand enough to join her. All they saw was the garden fence leaning over. Samantha had been so fearful of having to leave her home that she hadn't even fathomed that they might not be safe inside. Drawn curtains and locked windows hadn't meant a damn.

The monsters found us anyway.

A fence post snapped. An entire panel gave way, hopping out of its gravel board and falling flat onto the grass. In the panel's place stood a dozen of her former neighbours, some still recognisable as the people they'd been, others little more than fungus-covered abominations. Among them stood a separate creature, something larger and more obscene. Hideously misshapen. A single massive eyeball floated in its middle. Open-mouthed disembodied heads hung in clusters from its torso.

Matthew and Zoe started screaming, and Samantha had to force herself not to do the same. She couldn't afford to be afraid. She needed to be brave.

For the first time in my life, I have to be truly brave.

"Okay, children, it's time to leave. Let's head on over to the front door, shall we? That's it now. Quickly."

"My soos," said Matthew.

"Forget about your shoes and coats, pet. Just move with me, okay? Take my hand. That's it. Keep moving."

Matthew and Tammy shared her left hand while Zoe had her right, but Samantha had to loose them all while she turned the key in the front door and unlocked the deadbolt. Their frightened quaking caused her to quickly regrab their hands and open the door with her shoeless foot. How the hell was she going to keep them safe? How far did she need to take them?

Where do I go?

The sunlight hurt Samantha's eyes. She had to blink before she could see. Fighting the urge to wet her knickers, she leapt over the doorstep and onto the pavement outside. Whatever safety she had convinced herself existed in her home had now completely evaporated. She looked left and right, but all she saw was monsters. They filled the road, whipping their inhuman, tentacle-like arms and lashing out at the air. They stared at her in silence.

Hell had taken over Choirikell.

2

A nt Man 2. *That was the last film we saw. Sophie had a hotdog with onions. I had popcorn. We shared a giant Pepsi.*

That can't be the last movie we ever see together. I need to get to her. There needs to be more. More of a life with her by my side. A future.

My heart is breaking. No, not breaking. Half of it's missing.

Ant Man 2. *Fuck.*

"They cannae keep us here," said Cameron, stomping back and forth inside the wide-pitched tent like an angry bull. Wearing a thin blue paper gown, he looked somewhat absurd. The pitter-patter of rain against the canvas walls created a drumbeat to fill the silence between his words.

Ryan sat on his springy cot bed, looking equally ridiculous in his own matching gown. "Calm down, mate. Getting wound up ain't gunna fix anything, is it?"

"Oh, come on, English, grow some balls. These fascists only understand one thing – a good smack in the gob."

Miles groaned on the cot beside Ryan's. His head bandaged and his wounded eye hid beneath a fresh white pad. "They're nae *fascists*, Cameron. For heaven's sake, they're dealing with a crisis as best they can. They've kept us all safe, haven't they?"

"Aye. Barely."

Ryan agreed with Miles. While being placed under quarantine for the last three days hadn't been fun, they were still better off than they had been. Whenever a green came within a hundred metres of the camp, soldiers quickly dispatched it, rifles cracking once or twice every hour. It made sleeping a challenge, but it was nice to know they were being watched over. On the other hand, Ryan could also understand Cameron's frustration. For one thing, they were freezing. The small propane heater in the tent wasn't enough, and they had to bundle themselves in scratchy blankets like a tent full of mummies. Several bonfires burned outside, keeping away some of the chill, but the paper gowns they wore were woefully inadequate. Ryan shivered constantly. The only thing he had on beneath the thin blue material was his boxer shorts, and a multitude of medical dressings covering his many wounds.

He still struggled to comprehend what he had been through. For days he had done little except eat and sleep. His entire body had ached to the point of paralysis, and he had discovered blood in his urine. Only in the last twenty-four hours had he truly begun to feel well again, and much of it was due to the medical attention the army had provided. His missing toe had been stitched, his gashed forearm bandaged, and a regular stream of painkillers was very much appreciated. Ryan couldn't complain too harshly. He was alive.

Aaron sat on the cot opposite Ryan's. He swigged from an energy drink and gave a bemused smirk. "What are you going to do, Cameron? Go out and fight the army? Or maybe you're going to take your chances with the greens?"

"If I have tae, I will."

"Don't be an idiot," said Tom. He was at the rear of the tent, sitting furthest from the entrance flap. He had spoken very little in the past few days, spending most of his time with his nose buried inside the various paperbacks provided to them. Ryan had finished a couple of Andy McNab books, but he wasn't much of a reader. His mind kept wandering.

"Shut yer face, Poshie," said Cameron.

Tom rolled his eyes. "Delightful. I'm just saying you shouldn't look a gift horse in the mouth. We're lucky to be alive. We should be thanking our hosts, not criticising them."

"I quite agree," said a new voice, entering the tent through the flap. It was Lieutenant Holloway, the quarantine 'liaison'. A tall, reedy-limbed man with short dark hair greying at the temples, he checked in on them once or twice a day. "This will all be over soon," he told them. "You just need to remain patient a short while longer."

"How long?" Cameron demanded.

"Difficult to say. We still need to be sure you're not infected."

"We're not," said Tom, crossing his legs across his mattress. "Everyone is clearly fine."

Aaron spoke up, pointing a finger at the officer's face and drawing a circle in the air. "You're not wearing your mask. If you still thought we were infectious, you'd still have it on."

"Yeah," said Ryan, realising his brother had a point. "Not to mention it's been three days. The infection works a lot faster than that."

Tom nodded. "I've been checking myself in the shower every day and there's no sign of fungus."

Cameron smirked and made an obscene gesture. "Aye, he's been spending plenty o' time checking himself in the shower, that one."

Tom rolled his eyes and lay back on his cot, muttering under his breath.

Holloway sighed and leant up against one of the mobile dressers placed inside the tent. He gave them a shrug. "Doctor Gerard and I are ninety-nine per cent sure you're all going to be just fine, but until he gives the word, you're to remain in quarantine. I understand your frustrations, but please—"

"Feck off," said Cameron. "When are ye gunna tell us what's going on, eh? What the hell *is* this thing?"

"I'm not at liberty to say."

Miles groaned. "No one owns the truth, Lieutenant. We have a right to know."

Holloway sucked at his teeth, appearing to mull it over. In the last three days, he had become more and more casual around them. When they had first been placed in quarantine, he'd been curt and authoritarian, uniform crisp and a pistol always at his side. Now, the top two buttons of his shirt were open and his pistol rested in its holster. He had also gone a day or two without shaving, salt 'n' pepper stubble all over his hollow cheeks. "Look, to tell you the truth, gentlemen, we're not entirely sure what we're dealing with. There are theories, of course, but nothing that's been agreed upon."

"Then give us some of the leading theories," said Miles. When Holloway opened his mouth to argue, the vicar cut him off with a heartfelt, "*Please.*"

It seemed to do the trick because Holloway nodded slowly and gave a reply. "Terrorism is obviously the number one suspicion. Some kind of biological warhead deployed from a low orbit or an advanced stealth craft. We wouldn't place it in the realms of likelihood for most of our traditional enemies, but plenty of rogue groups in Russia desire worldwide anarchy. Not to mention chemistry is one of the Kremlin's favourite pastimes."

Aaron stared at Holloway suspiciously. "But you don't really believe that, do you?"

Holloway cleared his throat and ran a hand through his greying hair. His eyes were a light colour, green or blue, but the baggy flesh beneath them was almost black. "I suppose I *don't* believe it."

"Why not?" asked Tom, sitting back up on his cot and placing his paperback down on the pillow.

"Because Moscow is in bad shape, too. This thing has cropped up everywhere from Eastern Europe to the Gulf of Mexico. That might leave China as the culprit, but it would be a reckless move for a nation that's already winning."

Cameron grumbled. "Feckin' China."

"Time zones," said Aaron. Everybody looked at him, so he said it again. "Time zones."

Tom frowned a little condescendingly. "What are you talking about?"

Aaron was clearly still in the midst of thinking, but he shared his theory as it came to him. He looked at Holloway. "You said the Gulf of Mexico and Eastern Europe, right? That's, like, half the globe."

Holloway folded his arms and seemed ready to listen. "More or less,"

"Then it might have come from space, just like I've been saying." Everybody groaned, but Aaron protested. "No, just listen to me for a minute, okay? If something was fired at the Earth from space, it would only hit one side of the globe, right? Probably slightly less than that. Think about throwing pebbles at a beach ball. The pebbles couldn't hit the back of it, could they? What if aliens launched something from space at the Earth?"

"Ye mean the corkscrews?" said Cameron. He was usually the first to criticise Aaron's theories, but he seemed to take them seriously for once.

Aaron nodded excitedly. "Yes! What if the corkscrews were bullets fired at us from space?"

"More like seeds," said Cameron, "to grow that feckin' fungus everywhere."

"Payloads," said Aaron. "Biological warfare."

There was a moment of silence while everyone imagined a scenario where Aaron was right, but Ryan still found it hard to believe in aliens. Plus, there was something that concerned him more than his brother's wild theories. "Why aren't you saying anything?" he asked Holloway. "Why are you allowing my brother to get carried away instead of telling him he's wrong?"

"Because he's right," said Holloway with a shrug. Everyone

gasped, but he quickly put a hand up to quiet them. "He's right about the time zone thing. There have been over ten thousand of what you call 'corkscrews' identified across Europe, Africa, and the United States' east coast. We're assuming there are a whole deal more that sank beneath the Atlantic. Half the globe, more or less, just like young Mr Cartwright said. Each one loaded with oil-producing bugs."

Ryan leapt up from his cot. "I need to make a call right now." He'd been asking for a phone constantly over the last three days, but all he had been getting were excuses. Now things were worse than ever. This was not a localised event.

Half the globe...

Thousands of corkscrews.

"As I keep telling you, Mr Cartwright," said Holloway, his hand moving ever so slightly towards his pistol, "all lines are currently down. I cannot fulfil your request."

Ryan realised he was shaking. He had known things were bad, but half the globe? "I-I don't fucking believe you. I think this is all bullshit."

"Aye," said Cameron. "He's lying to us."

Holloway stood up straight. "Have you seen anyone in this camp use a radio or a mobile phone? Nothing is working, my friends. Nothing electrical, anyway. We're lucky a few of our older trucks still start, or we'd be completely cut off up here. Our information is received and delivered by hand."

"Phones work in a power cut," said Miles. "They dinnae need electricity."

"Quite right, Vicar, but the exchanges they run on do. Things went digital some time ago. The entire grid in this area was wiped out by the magnetic pulse when the first payloads hit. We're having to send messengers back and forth to Edinburgh to keep the crisis committee updated."

"Manchester," said Ryan. "What about Manchester?"

"Manchester is fine. The corkscrews fell over a period of ten hours from a single vector. The Earth's rotation during those ten hours is what led to the scattering across time zones. Manchester managed to avoid being hit, as did the entirety of Belgium from what I've heard. Lucky blighters."

"Feckin' EU," said Cameron. "Feckin' Brussels."

"So I wasn't completely correct then," said Aaron. "The corkscrews came in a stream like machine-gun fire, not scattered like a shotgun blast."

Holloway winked at him. "I appreciate a good firearm analogy, lad. You were close enough to earn points, let's put it that way."

"You swear Manchester is okay?" Ryan demanded. He couldn't see why the officer would lie to him, but it felt like home was on another planet and getting further and further away. He needed to know that Sophie and his mam were okay. "Please, just be honest with me."

"I *have* been honest with you, Mr Cartwright. The nearest corkscrew landed in Staffordshire, a dozen or so miles north of Stoke. Only one cluster landed north of the Scottish border, and we're sitting on it. There's a safe zone being set up between the Highlands and the upper part of the East Midlands, but..." He trailed off. Cameron stepped up to the officer, possibly trying to intimidate him, but Holloway showed little concern. He finished what he'd been about to say. "It's a shitshow everywhere else. London and the South East are apparently a war zone. East Anglia, too. Wales and the South West are allegedly faring a little better, but the only part of the country completely unaffected is the buffer zone between here and Staffordshire. A majority of the UK's operations are now being run from Holyrood. First Minister Pike is running the show for now."

Cameron whooped with joy. "Finally, some good news."

Ryan glared at him. "Are you fookin' serious?"

"Oh, stop yer whinging, English. Ye heard the man, Manchester's fine. In fact, it sounds like yer folks won the lottery."

"He's right," said Aaron glumly. "I can hardly believe it, but if

Manchester is okay when almost everywhere else isn't, we really are lucky. Mam and Sophie are okay."

"I don't see any of this as luck," said Ryan, gripping his cot mattress to keep from leaping up in a panic. His heart thudded back and forth between his spine and ribcage.

Holloway rubbed at the dark bags beneath his eyes and grunted. "Look, we're doing everything we can to recover from this, okay, but the biggest crisis facing the nation is panic. The nation is looting and rioting and failing to stay indoors. Things would get dealt with a hell of a lot sooner if people remained calm and just followed orders. That is why I'm asking to you to be patient."

"I need to speak to my fiancée," said Ryan. He was begging now.

Holloway took a weary breath inwards. "Okay, Mr Cartwright, here's what I'll do. What's left of Westminster is travelling up the Irish Sea to form an assembly in Liverpool. I'm due to send an intelligence update there tomorrow as soon as my messengers return from Edinburgh. If you pen a letter, I'll see if I can get it delivered to your family on their way home."

"Are you serious?"

"No promises. My men won't take unnecessary risks to deliver a letter, but if Manchester is still in the clear, they may be willing to take a brief detour to check on your family. The roads are closed to non-essential traffic anyway. Getting about isn't as time-consuming as it used to be."

Ryan got up and shook the officer's hand. "Thank you, sir."

"Can I write a letter too?" asked Aaron. "It's, um, to the same address. Our mam."

Holloway nodded. "Of course. Grubs up in about an hour, okay? Doctor Gerard is busy in the infirmary, but he'll be by to check on you shortly. Are you all feeling well?"

"Never been better," said Cameron sarcastically. His fuzzy ginger beard had grown out slightly and gave him a roguish appearance.

Miles waved a hand to quiet him down. "We appreciate the update, Lieutenant. For a jailer, yer worse than some but not as bad as others."

Holloway raised a bushy peppery eyebrow. "I'll take that as a compliment. Oh, as to your earlier request, Vicar, I've decided to grant it. You can visit your friends in the other tent after dinner. Just sit tight and someone will take you over."

Everyone sighed with relief. It had been a while since they'd got good news, and they had all missed the girls.

Shortly after the army had seized them, Ryan and the others had been separated from Fiona and Chloe. They had tried protesting, but at that point the army wasn't messing around. They had approached wearing biohazard suits and wielding nasty-looking shotguns with black stocks, making it abundantly clear that it was in everyone's best interests to do exactly what they were told. Ryan had only known Chloe and Fiona for a short while, but it felt wrong being away from them. He dared even to think of them as *friends*.

With Officer Holloway having departed the tent, everyone began their debriefing. It was what they always did whenever they learned something new. They were a team. Miles shook his head and closed his good eye. Doing the sign of the cross, he spoke solemnly. "It is everywhere, as we feared."

"Aye," said Cameron. "Where's yer God now, Vicar? If this is an alien invasion, or the end of the world, where is He?"

Miles sighed, his eye still closed. "Please, Cameron Pollock, I dinnae need ye to question ma beliefs. I can do that all on ma own. I always swore never to doubt the Lord, but this is a test perhaps beyond me. My soul weeps."

Cameron looked away awkwardly. "Yeah, um, all right. Chin up, Vicar, eh? No harm meant."

Ryan sat back on his cot, shivering beneath his paper gown. He grabbed some blankets and bundled them around himself. "We'll get through this somehow. We've made it this far, haven't we? It will all be okay so long as we keep looking after each other."

Cameron rolled his eyes. "Ye mean until ye jump ship at the first chance to head south? Yoo English boys ain't gunna stick aroond here."

"I need to get home, Cameron. I'm not going to pretend otherwise."

"Me too," said Tom. "There are people we care about. Ryan isn't the only one with family and a partner."

"Aye," said Cameron, "but he's the only one who never shuts up aboot them. Sophie this, mam that. Gives ma arse an 'eadache."

Ryan glared. "Shut your face."

"We understand," said Miles, smiling compassionately at Ryan while holding up a hand to stop Cameron's inevitable reply. "Dinnae feel even a wee bit guilty aboot it, all right? Home is where ye must be."

"You should come with us," said Aaron. "Manchester is safe. You heard Holloway."

Cameron scoffed. "He dinnae say it was safe, little English. He said it didn't get hit by the corkscrews. What do ye think people are gunna be acting like with the world all around them on fire? They'll be running aboot like heidless chickens. Nah, it's safer here, out in the hills. A true Scot can survive anything out in the wild."

Miles groaned. "Yer not William Wallace, so stop acting the prat. Ryan, I'm sure yer family are safe and sound, and that ye'll be reunited soon." He nodded at Aaron. "And if there's an offer of bed and board, I'd like to take ye up on it."

Ryan frowned. "You really want to head down to Manchester with us, Vicar? Aren't you needed here?"

"For what? Ye burned down ma feckin' church, and all my parishioners are... no longer Christian. If there's anything I can do to help, it's nae here on the edge of civilisation."

Ryan smiled. "If you hadn't let me and Aaron inside the

church that night, we wouldn't have made it. You're forever welcome at our home."

"We'd be glad to have you," said Aaron with a great beaming smile of his own.

"I would nae get ye hopes up, English," said Cameron. "We'll probably end the week with a bullet in our heids. If they were gunna let us go, they woulda done it already. I reckon we need to get our bums oot the windae soon as we can."

"Don't be ridiculous," said Tom at the back of the tent. He eyed them over the top of his book. "Not all of us are suicidal."

"I reckon Cameron's right," said Aaron. "I can't see them just letting us walk away with a pat on the back."

Ryan showed his surprise with a gasp. Agreeing with Cameron was rarely a wise idea, and he thought his brother was smarter than that. "We try to leave, they'll shoot us where we stand. Don't let him get inside your head, Aaron."

"He's not. I agree with him. Holloway knows we're not infected, so why hasn't he let us go? You heard how bad things are, and things are only going to get worse. The army can do whatever it wants and no one will be around to stop it."

"Too right," said Cameron. "Least one o' yoo English is thinking clearly."

Miles sighed. "Let's nae act rashly. We're allowed to see Fiona and Chloe later. We should focus on that. I've been worried for them."

"Me too," said Ryan. "Tell you the truth, there's another person I've been worried about as well."

"Helen," said Cameron with a curt nod. "Aye, she's been on ma mind too."

"You think she could still be alive?"

"Nah, she would have come and sliced yer neck open by now."

A knot formed in Ryan's stomach as he pictured the woman's baleful glare. "She blamed me for Andy's death. *Am* I responsible? Am I to blame?"

Cameron sneered, but he seemed to think about it at the same time. Eventually, his sneer dissipated and he shook his head. "Yer nae more to blame than any o' us, English. We all failed to protect that little lad."

Miles nodded. "The only person responsible for this is whoever sent those corkscrews falling from the skies. Yer a good lad, Ryan. Forgive thyself, eh?"

Ryan felt tears forming, but it was nothing new. He'd been so tired and weak these last few days that the merest bad thought could summon sobs deep from within. While his wounds were healing, his mind still throbbed with infirmity. His energy levels were on the floor. All the same, he felt a spark of happiness to have the approval of his new acquaintances. "Thank you, Miles. You too, Cameron."

Cameron nodded. "Aye."

Miles lay back on his cot and adjusted his eye patch. "Now, let's enjoy a wee bit o' silence while we have it. They'll be plenty of time for worrying later."

Ryan lay back on his cot, pulling the blankets over him. *Later, yes, but there's no time like the present.*

DOCTOR GERARD ENTERED the tent looking more like a patient than a carer. He was a soldier, too, and wore a set of camouflage fatigues stained by mud and blood in several places, but he never seemed to carry a weapon. Like Holloway, his collar and top buttons were open, and he wore a dark blue T-shirt underneath. His ashen skin suggested he hadn't slept in days, and he struggled to carry his heavy case of medical equipment into their tent. The sleeves of his fatigues were rolled up, revealing thick black hair at odds with his balding head. Usually, he had a clipboard with him, but he seemed to have forgotten it tonight. "Good evening, gentleman," he said in his usual, well-spoken tone, but this time there was the slightest of Scottish twangs. "Is everyone all right?"

Miles went to speak, but Cameron got there first. "Ye look like shite on an ice cream cone, Doc. Maybe it's yoo what should be lying doon in here."

The doctor chuckled weakly. "I'm not ill. Stressed and exhausted, perhaps, but I don't have the luxury of being ill. How are the five of you feeling? Any symptoms I should know about? Miles, how is your eye? I've brought you some more pain relief."

"It's nae hurting as much," said Miles. "This morning I could even open it a little to see."

"That's wonderful news. Hopefully you'll recover full use of it in time."

Cameron folded his arms and perched on the edge of his bed. "We're as right as rain, Doc. Go tell Major Reid to let us oota here."

Doctor Gerard blinked slowly behind his wire-rimmed spectacles. "I've already suggested most of your restrictions be lifted. I'm confident none of you are infected. In fact, your survival has proved informative. Removing your infected toe was clearly successful, Mr Cartwright, as was Miss Floros applying heat to her infected wound. Battlefield medicine at its finest."

Cameron tittered. "Ye talking aboot Ryan holding her arm against a coal burner? Is that what counts fer treatment these days?"

"Apparently so. Miss Floros is doing very well as a result. Did Holloway inform you he has cleared it so you can mix between the tents? Your clothes have been washed and dried. I'll have them brought to you momentarily. I'll see about having a second gas heater brought in as well. It's starting to get a little chilly in here."

It had started out chilly. Now it was bordering on downright freezing. Ryan didn't complain, though, because the thought of getting out of the thin blue gown and back into his own clothes was like a hundred Christmas presents at once. "Thank you, Doctor. I think we would all appreciate that very much."

"You're welcome. I understand this has been a difficult time. Your patience is appreciated."

Ryan gave the doctor a good hard look. Something was clearly off about him. He was usually a stern, dismissive man, but he had dropped the doctor–patient facade and was speaking to them in a strange, detached sort of way that almost made it seem like he didn't much care. His shoulders sagged and he seemed drowsy. Had he taken something to relax, or was he just exhausted as he said? Something clearly weighed on the man.

"What *is* this thing?" asked Aaron. "Do we know how to get rid of the fungus?"

To everyone's surprise, Doctor Gerard sat down on one of the cot beds. He took off his spectacles to rub at his eyes. "It's not a fungus, exactly, but it's not far off to say that it is. The organic compounds we've isolated are not in line with any species on record, but like a fungus it absorbs nutrients from its environment in order to grow. Rather than releasing airborne spores, however, it seems to spread via an oily substance that we're not yet fully educated about. Examined under a microscope, it appears to be some kind of mildly acidic substance, acting as a suspension for microscopic seeds. It's produced by a new and uncategorised species of bug, which makes it difficult to contain."

"Forget all that," said Cameron. "How do we kill the feckin' stuff?"

"Yes," said Tom, once again putting down his paperback. "You know how to kill it, right?"

"We've been experimenting exhaustively," said Gerard, "and there have been many promising discoveries. For instance, we have found that the organism is sensitive to alkaline conditions. That's good news, because much of our soil is slightly alkaline. It has been proven to slow the growth of the fungus, although only as a mild inhibitor. However, concentrated chemicals with a higher PH can outright destroy the organism. Bleach, for instance."

Cameron huffed. "Bleach? As in, what ye clean the shitter

with?"

The doctor nodded. "Exactly."

"Why are you telling us all this?" asked Aaron. "You haven't answered any of our questions like this before."

Miles nodded. "Holloway was uncharacteristically forthright too."

The doctor reached into his pocket and pulled out a pack of cigarettes. He didn't ask if anyone minded while he lit up – nor did he offer to share. After he had taken a deep drag, he yawned. "I don't see any purpose keeping you in the dark," he told them. "At first, we were worried about controlling the spread of information, but it's clearly going to be a while before any of us can send a text message or email. We're stuck on this hill together, so we might as well keep each other informed. Anyway, back to the matters at hand. I'm going to recommend for you to remain quarantined until morning. After that, you'll be fully cleared."

"So we can leave?" asked Ryan.

"I'm afraid not. Movement of people is completely restricted – a necessity to keep this thing from spreading – but you'll be allowed to walk around camp in a responsible manner. It's not exactly Disneyland, but we have some activities to keep boredom at bay. You'll be better off than you have been."

"I really need to make it home to Manchester," said Ryan. "My fiancée is there. Me mam too."

"I understand. I have family in York that I would very much like to see, but it's not an option right now."

Ryan shrugged. "What if I just leave?"

"Then I expect you'd be shot."

Cameron spat. "Fascists."

Gerard's expression hardened, and his normally stern demeanour returned. "Desperate times demand desperate measures, gentlemen. Go back into the village and fend for yourselves if it suits you, but if not, I suggest you count yourselves lucky to be here under this camp's protection. Now, let me see to your wounds so I can be out of your hair."

Doctor Gerard changed everyone's dressings and administered pain relief, then stumbled out of the tent half-asleep. Five minutes later, a private arrived with everybody's freshly cleaned clothes. Ryan felt amazing getting back in his jeans, and the air's cold bite retreated slightly. There was no sign of a second gas heater though. He had also requested a pen and paper so he could write the letter to Sophie and his mam. He had finished it in ten minutes, the words spilling out onto the page in a way they never had before. While he had been writing, it was if they were there with him. He was speaking directly to them. Once the letter was finished, a deep emptiness had taken over him.

He hung his head in silence. Aaron moved beside him and wrapped an arm around his shoulders. "We'll make it home, bro. Eventually, we will."

"It's like being torn in two. If not for Mam and Sophie, I would happily stay here with a hundred armed soldiers protecting me."

"We dinnae need 'em," said Cameron. "We were doing fine on our own."

Ryan gawped. "Are you kidding me? There was barely anything of me left by the time the army came. Miles was nearly blinded. Fiona has third-degree burns, and Stewart and Gavin... well, they never even made it. Oh, and Tom is missing an earlobe. In fact, you're a jammy bastard, do you know that?"

Cameron chuckled but seemed confused. "Why am I?"

"Because you rush head first into danger every time there's trouble, and you're still in better shape than any of us."

"I got a mild concussion, English, or did ye forget?"

"After throwing yourself through a plate-glass window? Yeah, I remember."

"Desperate times demand desperate measures," said Miles, and everybody laughed.

"I have to admit," said Ryan, "you're a tough bastard, Cameron, even by Manchester standards."

Cameron smirked and seemed pleased with himself.

A high-pitched bell sounded three times, signalling dinner. The sudden, uncomfortably loud noise always made them jump, but it prompted the five of them to leap up excitedly from their cot beds. When the army had first fed Ryan, he had eaten for over an hour, a deep hole in him refusing to be filled. Now, seventy-two hours later, dinner time was still the best part of the day. The army truly did march on a full stomach.

Ryan limped outside, his brother beside him. Miles followed slowly behind the group, having grown clumsy since losing the use of one eye. Cameron marched to the front of the group, no doubt wanting to sit down first. It was getting darker, and the soldiers had already lit the camp's three large bonfires. Soon, a set of blinding floodlights would come to life, powered by a noisy petrol generator. The light rain had stopped for now, but it had left everything damp. It seemed that the Highlands was forever either damp or cold – or both.

The soldiers ate in a large gazebo near the centre of camp, but the 'patients' ate at small tables outside each of their tents. Fiona and Chloe were at the eastern edge of the camp, while the men were on the west. A couple of times, Ryan had spotted children and other women over on the east side, and he wondered how many other survivors had made it out of Choirikell.

In the last few days, the soldiers had pushed up as far as the village's petrol station. There, they had set up razor wire and sandbags in a defensive line, using megaphones morning, noon, and night to call out for survivors. They never proactively searched the village, though, and their primary concern seemed to be keeping anything green from getting out. It gave Ryan a slim hope that the army might be able to control the crisis. This might not be the end of the world.

Ryan sat down at the designated picnic table and waited for dinner to be served. Usually, he and the others would be shivering in their gowns and wrapped in blankets, but tonight that they were finally back in their old clothes. Miles once again had his dog collar, and Cameron was back in his cargo trousers and burnt orange jumper. Tom seemed strangely overdressed in his pastel shirt and chinos.

The cook who delivered their food wore a mask, as did many other soldiers around camp, but many more did not. Rather than mandatory, masks seemed optional, which could only be a good sign. Ryan had never considered the fungus – or whatever it was – to be airborne, but the fact the soldiers were being less cautious all but confirmed it. It was the oil that was infectious. That, and the deadly talons hanging from the green's tendrils.

The chef took food from a trolley and placed it down on the table. Then he left. Baked beans, mashed potato, and what was either chicken or fish goujons. Not high-class fare, by any means, but plenty of it and all piping hot. As usual, Cameron tucked in first, scooping a huge dollop of mashed potato onto his plastic plate followed by lashings of baked beans and a fistful of goujons. His mouth was full before anyone else even picked up a plate.

Ryan piled his own feast and made a start. No matter what was happening in the world, eating always felt good. It was a moment where he could concentrate on fulfilling one of his body's needs and forget about all the others. It shut off his worries. For a while.

They ate in silence, peering around the dusky camp with interest. Soon, the three enormous bonfires would be lit, providing both light and warmth during the frigid night. Every morning, when Ryan left his tent for a shower or to go to the toilet, the camp would seem to have changed. The dozens of small green and brown tents, along with another dozen large white ones, appeared to subtly shift locations. Maybe it was all in his mind. Or perhaps it was a way of keeping the soldiers busy.

There was a large space in the centre of camp where soldiers played football or worked out, and several smaller areas for playing cards and chatting. Many of the soldiers seemed to sit around reading books and magazines when not guarding the perimeter, and many tapped futilely at broken tablets and mobile phones. Up near the petrol station, two dozen guards kept watch at all times, crouched behind sandbags with their rifles aimed ahead. The officer in charge was Major Reid, but he rarely appeared outside of a large square tent at the rear of camp. Ryan hadn't seen the man at all in the last day or two.

"Hey, look," said Aaron, pointing. "There's Fiona and Chloe."

The girls were coming out of their tent on the opposite side of the camp. Seeing them at mealtimes was the only confirmation they had that the women were okay. They both waved, as they usually did, then sat down.

"They seem to be all right," said Aaron. "You think we can go over?"

Miles frowned. "*After* dinner, we were told. We should wait for the go-ahead first."

Aaron nodded.

"Sod that," said Cameron, and he stood up with his heaped plate. "I'm goin' over."

Ryan grimaced but found himself standing up as well, knowing he would have to back Cameron up one way or another. Embarrassingly, he almost tripped when he caught his wounded foot on the chair leg and yelled in pain, but the table kept him from falling. Soon all five of them were on their feet and marching across camp. Tom, however, was doing his best to get them to sit back down. "Are you incapable of avoiding trouble?" he complained. "It's like being stuck with a bunch of ten-year-olds."

"Quiet yer mouth, Poshie."

"I'm just saying it's a bad idea. We're going to end up getting—"

A corporal – if that's what the two chevrons on his arm meant – stepped in their way. The shaved-headed soldier was unarmed but held out a stiff arm. There was a round scar on his left cheek that looked like a cigarette burn. "Where ye think yer going?"

"We've been cleared to mix with the women," said Miles, giving an answer before Cameron could.

"Sit back down at ye table."

"Feck off," said Cameron, squaring up to the corporal, who didn't seem at all worried by the fact he was a foot shorter.

"Sit down, right now, all o' ye. I'll nae ask again."

Cameron remained where he was. "Then *dinnae* feckin' ask."

"Right, ye wanna play games? That's all right wi' me." The corporal reached out and grabbed Cameron by the wrist.

Big mistake. Huge.

"Feck off, ye bawbag." Cameron leant in and headbutted the corporal right on the nose. The soldier reared back, clutching his face and squealing. Blood started to flow. Several soldiers at nearby tables leapt up. Some had pistols, and they wasted no time in pointing them. Ryan put his hands above his head and exchanged worried glances with Miles and Aaron. It had only been a matter of time before Cameron landed them all in boiling water. It looked like the time had arrived.

"Ye've done it, dow. Ye're a deb mam." The corporal's words were thick with blood. "Ye're deb!"

A new voice shouted. "Corporal Kay! Report to the infirmary at once!"

The soldier turned, still clutching his face and trying to stem the blood gushing from his nose. "Lieutenant Holloway, sir? Dis pribna just attabbed me."

Holloway marched across camp, prompting the standing soldiers to sit back down and avert their eyes. The lieutenant positioned himself in front of his corporal and put his hands on his hips. "They are not *prisoners*, Kay, they are civilians under our care. Go to the infirmary, at once, before I put you there."

Kay grumbled to himself but marched away without argument. A nearby soldier stood up to help him. He glared at Cameron from beneath a black woollen beanie hat.

"We're sorry, Lieutenant," said Miles, but Holloway ignored him and whirled to face Cameron.

"Assault one of my soldiers again and I'll shoot you between the eyes. Do you understand me?" Cameron sneered and refused to answer. Holloway whipped his pistol out of its holster and pointed it at his face. "Do you understand me?"

Cameron didn't move. He glared at Holloway across the barrel of his pistol.

Ryan tugged at Cameron's arm. "Come on, man, just say you understand."

After a tense moment, where it seemed entirely possible that Holloway might actually shoot Cameron, the big Scot folded his arms and looked away. Fortunately, it was enough for Holloway to reholster his pistol and address the rest of them. "I am in no mood for games, gentlemen. Do not make me babysit you."

"We're sorry, Lieutenant," said Miles again. "We just wanted to see our friends. Ye said we could."

"I *said* you could see them after dinner." He looked around camp. "Dinner seems to still be in session, wouldn't you agree?" Ryan went to speak, but the lieutenant didn't allow him to. His cheeks were red, his face an oil painting of rage, yet he remained fully in control. "Do not mistake your importance here. My duty here is to keep all hazardous materials from spreading south. That is my sole concern. Endanger my mission and you shall find yourselves on very dangerous ground. It would be no bother at all to write a report saying we found no survivors in this village. Easiest thing in the world."

No one said anything, but they all nodded to show that they understood the threat – everyone except Cameron, who remained looking the other way. After a moment, Miles dared to speak. "Ye have ma word, Lieutenant. We'll behave."

"I *am* behaving," said Tom. "It's only one of us who keeps causing problems."

"*Cameron* will behave," Miles adjusted. "I'll make sure of it."

Holloway glared at the side of Cameron's head. "I'm unconvinced."

"We'll keep him on a tight lead," said Ryan. "We promise."

And he'll probably chew through that lead and bite the postman, but at least we'll have tried.

Holloway's shoulders lowered. His angry expression softened. "Well, go on then. Go see your ladies."

Miles clasped his hands together in a prayer gesture and tipped his fingers at the officer. "You're a gracious man, Lieutenant Holloway. Thank you."

"Just don't make me regret it. My patience is nearing its end."

Cameron went to speak, but Ryan bumped him in the back to get him moving. The five of them made their way across camp, while a hundred pairs of eyes condemned them. Soldiers stuck together, and Cameron had just nutted one in the face. A horrendously stupid thing to do, but it was too late to take it back. Ryan suddenly felt less protected and more endangered.

When Fiona saw them approaching, she stood up from the table and grinned. Her hair was up in a ponytail, revealing her missing left earlobe, which Ryan found curious. Maybe it had happened while she was in prison, but right now it wasn't important. He hurried over and gave her a great big hug. It was unsettling how much he'd missed her.

"It's good to see you up close again," said Fiona.

Ryan eased out of the hug. "Yeah, you too. How you doing?"

"Could be worse."

The women's tent was closer to one of the bonfires, and Ryan shuddered as the heat warmed his back. "Could be better, too, though, huh?"

"Have they said it's okay for you to come over here?" asked Chloe. She was still sitting, knife and fork still in her hands. Her plate was piled high with beans and mashed potato, but no goujons. Her hair was in a ponytail like Fiona's, and without her dark eye make-up she looked like a completely different person. Like the men, the two women had also been given back their own clothes. Both were dressed in dark clothes, and Fiona's tattoo sleeves were on display – except for the ruined Japanese oni on her forearm that was now covered by a fresh white bandage.

"Holloway just allowed it," said Miles. "Doctor Gerard has given us the all-clear."

"Ninety-nine per cent all-clear," Aaron added. "There's still a chance one of us might turn into a monster."

Chloe chuckled. "I feel fine. Unless you count boredom as an illness?"

"I definitely do. I must have read the same magazine a dozen times."

"We're healthy as a field o' horses," said Cameron, rolling his eyes. "Shoulda been cleared days ago."

Fiona motioned back towards the other side of the camp. "What was all the commotion about back there? Something happen?"

Tom grunted. "Just Cameron being Cameron. Maybe you can keep him under control, because we clearly can't."

Cameron grinned. "Aye, Poshie, ye cannae make a lapdog of me."

"I would have you put down."

"Everybody, sit," said Fiona, motioning to the folding chairs around the table. "Hey, Miles, how's your eye?"

Miles placed his plate on the table and took a seat. "Healing well. Might not lose any sight."

"That's great!"

"Aye."

Cameron pulled a face. "Yer dinnae wannae lift that eye patch, though. Looks like an inmate's arsehole under there."

Fiona grimaced, and Ryan wondered if it was the vulgarity or the memories of being locked up in one of Her Majesty's prisons. He still found it hard to imagine her behind bars.

"Cameron's as charming as ever, as you can see," said Tom, picking up his fork and tucking into his mashed potato.

Everyone chuckled, even Cameron. He and Tom had seemed to have found a way of tolerating each other. It involved a lot of insults.

Three children and a couple of older women sat at a separate picnic table nearby. They were chatting amongst themselves glumly. The children seemed to be in shock. Ryan nodded to them as he picked up his cutlery. "Who are they?"

"Mavis and Ruth," said Chloe. "They were driving through the village when the corkscrews hit. Spent two days hiding oot in their car. Made a run for it when they heard the soldiers calling through the megaphone. They're tough old nags."

"Aye," said Cameron. "I had a fair few clips round the ear from the both of 'em when I were a bairn."

"What about the children?" asked Miles. "Is that little Matthew Meadows I see over there?"

Chloe shrugged. "No idea. The soldiers brought them in last night. The poor wee ones are probably traumatised."

"I'm glad other people made it," said Aaron. "It felt like we were the only ones."

Fiona sighed. "Can't say a lot did, though, can we? All the people in the village, and this is all that's left? I can't sleep at night, thinking about all those who never made it."

"Not to mention the soldiers firing their guns at all times of night," said Chloe, poking at her mashed potatoes. "Right feckin' racket."

"Keeps us alive," said Ryan. "So I'll take it."

Chloe nodded. "Aye, I suppose yer right."

"I just wish they'd head into the village and take care of things," said Fiona. "There could be other survivors in need of rescue."

"Like at the pub," said Aaron.

Fiona nodded. "Exactly. I'd like to meet those hooligans face to face. They nearly blinded Miles."

"Dinnae get angry on my behalf," he said. "Forgiveness is good for the soul."

Fiona sighed. "I know you're right, but still..."

"You're a good man," said Tom, shaking his head at Miles. "I don't think I could forgive. I'm still fuming about my ear being bitten off by a so-called friend who is now resting in peace." He tapped at his bandaged earlobe. "My Amanda is probably going to be quite disgusted."

"What good did anger ever do for anybody, lad? Let it go."

Tom nodded thoughtfully. He didn't mention Amanda or his family much, and Ryan wondered how much he missed them. Tom's father was a stern man who always demanded a lot from his son, and Ryan wouldn't be surprised if Tom was enjoying a break from being under his thumb.

He's never had to survive on his own. He's never even had to make a decision for himself before.

Ryan started to eat. It was great seeing the girls again, but now that the reunion was complete, it was back to old routines. He didn't want to miss the chance to fill his belly before another evening of mind-numbing isolation.

Everyone chatted idly between mouthfuls of food. Chloe revealed herself to be vegan, which caused Cameron to snort, but he changed his attitude when he realised it left more fish goujons for him. The food was plainer than previous nights, which had included a lively paella and a beef-laden stew, but it wasn't bad. The potato and goujons reminded Ryan of the school meals he had eaten as a kid. Happier times by far.

He looked around the camp, observing the expressions of various soldiers, predominantly male. Everyone seemed unusually tense tonight; less chatty, more glum. Some of the men glared at Ryan and his companions, while others ate their food in silence. One soldier, however, would not take his eyes off of Ryan.

With his shaven head and standard-issue green jumper, the man was barely distinguishable from his brothers in arms, but his ashen skin gleamed with sweat and his mouth was half-open, almost gaping. His dark, slitted eyes shot laser beams right across the camp, targeted right at Ryan.

"What is that guy's problem?" Ryan mumbled to himself.

Miles heard him. "Ryan? What's wrong?"

"That soldier over there. He's glaring at me. Look!"

There was a moment's silence while everyone at the table

sought out the glaring soldier. Cameron spotted him first. "What's he feckin' looking at? I ought to show him ma arse."

"Stay seated, Cameron Pollock," warned Miles. "We're already on thin ice after yer earlier performance."

Cameron grumbled. "Well, what's his problem? Why's he just sitting there, staring at us?"

As if in response, the soldier leapt to his feet, still glaring at Ryan. In fact, he was staring so hard that his eyes bulged. The left popped so far out that it came loose and dangled on his cheek. Inside the empty socket was a clump of green fuzz.

Oh shit!

"Kermit," someone shouted, and the camp exploded into life. A cascade of movement emanated from the table where the infected soldier stood.

"Get back," someone yelled.

"Dinnae touch him!"

Guards appeared from everywhere, aiming rifles but unable to get a clear shot off with so many rushing bodies in the way. The infected man had clearly been sitting with friends, because one of the other soldiers failed to move away. Instead, he reached out a hand to help. The infected soldier turned his one good eye on his friend and raised both arms as if to go in for a hug, but then he slapped the man hard across the face. The startled soldier stumbled backwards against the table, clutching his face in shock.

Thunder roared.

Bullets riddled the infected soldier's torso. Blood and greasy chunks of flesh filled the air. He flopped like a fish, sprawling over a chair and disappearing out of sight. The three enormous bonfires cast hundreds of flickering shadows across the camp, but then a dozen high-powered floodlights came to life and those shadows raced away.

At some point, Ryan and his companions had stood up. Each of them stared, wide-eyed and in absolute shock at the carnage that had just taken place. The camp was abuzz, soldiers grabbing rifles and barking orders at each other. Ryan saw scuffles erupt in several other areas of camp. More rifle fire cracked.

"Jesus Christ," said Cameron.

Miles winced. "How many people are infected?"

"We're nae safe here," said Chloe, horror flooding her face. "We never were."

Fiona wrapped an arm around her. "Stay calm. Let them handle it."

And handle it they did. Once the soldiers realised the threat, they responded swiftly. Without hesitation, they dispatched the infected men and women with calm, lethal shots to the chest and head. Blood stained the air, exposed by the shafts of light spilling from the floodlights. Men yelled military codes mixed with obscenities. Then, less than a minute later, it was all over.

As the chaos settled down, several casualties revealed themselves. Half a dozen soldiers clutched wounds that were probably already teeming with infection. Some were deathly silent. Others panicked.

Lieutenant Holloway appeared beside Ryan, a pair of privates flanking him. "Back inside your tent. Now!" The officer's authority was so legitimate and forceful that not even Cameron argued. They hurried inside the women's tent and didn't make a sound. It was exactly the same as the men's tent – two rows of springy cot beds and a pair of mobile drawer units – but there was also a changing screen at the back.

Holloway went in after them. "Are any of you hurt?"

"No," said Ryan. "How did this—"

"Remain here until told otherwise." Holloway turned and left. The two guards stood outside the flap.

Fiona cleared some magazines off of one of the cot beds and hopped up, crossing her legs on the mattress. "Might as well make yourselves at home. I think it's going to be a long night."

Or a very, very short one, thought Ryan.

The infection is inside the camp.

3

A few days ago, everyone had dared move down to the pub's ground floor. While they still slept upstairs, there was more room to spread out and generally 'live' downstairs. Thick green curtains covered the windows and they had barricaded the doors with tables. A heavy industrial glass cleaner blocked the fire exit in the kitchen. They kept the darkness at bay with a smattering of candles that would probably run out before the week was through. All in all, they were safe, but they were also trapped. Yesterday had proven that.

Sam from the village had been calling out for help, three children in her care. Even though she had been right outside, no one in the pub had been able to reach her. They had tried, but they had failed. In fact, they had almost died. The greens had been attracted by Sam's cries, and they had been amassing outside ever since, but it was the arrival of the beast that had kept them from helping the woman. It had seemingly arrived out of thin air, a great lumbering thing, and it had chased Sam and the children away just as they had been about to make it inside the pub. The thought of those three terrified children kept Helen from sleeping. She existed, today, in a cloudy haze.

Their faces reminded me of Andy's right at the end. I'd never seen him afraid before. Not like that.

Before his final moments in the church, the most frightened Helen had ever seen her daffodil was during a weekend break in Inverness. He'd been eating an ice cream when a big fat wasp had landed and settled on his hand. He had been stung the year before and had had a debilitating fear of them ever since. This wasp had perched on his tiny little hand for almost a minute, but it had seemed to last forever. Andy had looked at her in utter terror, waiting for her to take care of the situation, but she had done nothing. She had been too frightened of scaring the wasp and making it sting, so she had told Andy to stay still. He had taken it as a betrayal, his desperate eyes pleading with his mother and not understanding why she would not remove this dangerous animal from his hand. After the pest had finally flown away, Andy had thrown his ice cream and started to sob. She had hugged him, but she knew this was a moment he would never forget.

He's so sensitive.

Was. He was so sensitive.

Was...

Helen tried to think about something other than Andy as she sat alone in near darkness at one of the pub's small round tables, but his frozen, bloodless face would not leave her. Whenever she managed to turn her mind to something else, even for a second, a wave of realisation would crash over her and remind her, once again, that her daffodil was gone forever. In a surreal, dreadful kind of way, Andy had never even existed. He had never been real. A memory of a dream.

Dale was grieving too – she knew it – but instead of sitting in silence, trapped inside his own mind, he moved constantly, giving out orders and reminding everyone that it was 'his' pub. He busied himself by carving spears from chair legs or piling his exotic knife collection on the bar. Several times a day, he shouldered the shotgun that Helen knew had once belonged to his grandfather and marched around like a soldier.

Dale's family had lived in Choirikell for hundreds of years. His ancestors had built the pub, and the community hall listed his family name on a commemorative plaque. Dale's lineage was old and respected, but it had gone rotten the day his father, Leon Finley, had died. Dale had inherited the family's sizeable assets and started behaving like he owned the village – along with the people in it. He was a forty-year-old thug with more money than morals, and the fact she had once been in love with him was a puzzle. It had resulted in Andy, so it was something she would never regret, but it was not something she recalled fondly. All of the being cheated on, the insults, and the occasional black eye had only been worth it because of Andy.

Now Andy was dead, and she was once again back in Dale's clutches. She was as frightened of him now as she had ever been, but she gained comfort that his anger was at least pointed in other directions. If Dale ever got his hands on Ryan, there would be bloodshed. For that, she could at least be thankful.

I just want to be there to see it.

He brought those monsters to the church and watched them take away my daffodil. He took away everything I cared about. Who am I now?

Presently, Dale was taking out his anger on poor Ed McCulloch. The teenager was rushing back and forth through the shadows, gathering food supplies from the kitchen and gathering them up as speedily as he could. His baseball cap was half hanging off his head. Dale wanted to enforce rationing upon the group, which made sense, but he was being a total arse about it. The least he could do was wait until morning when they would all be able to see better.

"Hurry up, shithouse. I want this done!"

"I need a break," Ed pleaded. "I've been carrying boxes back and forth for an hour. I'm done in, pal."

"Quit yer greetin' and get it done, ye lazy sack o' shit."

Neat-haired Oliver Munson was leaning over the bar nearby, sorting packets of crisps. He was one of the smarter men in town, running an IT company from his home, but he was stupid enough to open his mouth now. "Come on, Dale. Give the lad a wee rest. There's nae rush, is there?"

Dale's expression turned dark, something Helen was regretfully familiar with. He strode up to Oliver and got in the man's face, almost nose to nose. "Yer in ma pub, pal. Ye nae like it, yer arse can get oot the windae."

Oliver leant back, trying to regain his personal space. When he spoke again, his voice quivered. "I-I'm just saying we have nothing but time on our hands, so just... just go a little easier, eh?"

Dale sneered, and everyone in the room watched in silence, seeing what he would do. There were thirteen people in their group altogether, but most tried to keep to themselves, not wanting to get shouted at or made to work. When Dale broke out in laughter, it probably shocked people more than if he had thrown a punch.

"Dinnae fret so much, Oliver-lad. Yer'll have yerself a coronary." Dale patted him on the back, hard enough to make him wince. "I suppose we can all afford to take a wee break if it'll keep yer from shittin' yer keks."

Oliver smiled thinly, clearly relieved. "That was all I were saying."

"Thank God." Ed dumped a box of peanuts onto a stool and sighed. His wobbly legs carried him over to a chair and he fell onto it. Helen pitied the lad. He was a good kid, but he would probably die a painful death in the not-too-distant future. They all would, but Ed sooner than others. The kid was weak.

The greens were everywhere outside. People could ration food and supplies all they wanted, but it wouldn't alter the fact they would eventually run out. Unless someone came to rescue them soon, starvation would continue to slither relentlessly towards them. Every day that passed made it less and less likely that help even existed. Whatever had inflicted itself upon Choirikell was larger than what they could see through the pub's windows. Maybe civilisation was in ruins. Maybe the world was full of murdered children just like Andy.

"Yer candle's getting low," said Shelly.

Helen looked up. "Huh?"

"Yer candle. It's nearly gone." Dale's barmaid, Shelly, was in her late-thirties, but her sun-ravaged skin made her look fifty. She'd spent most of her twenties working the club scenes in Spain, and if Helen was honest, she had no idea why the woman had ever come back. If Helen ever got out of the village, she would run a thousand miles and never look back. She had often dreamt of taking Andy to go live some place warm, and a recurring fantasy of hers involved meeting a French businessman and moving to his home in the south of France. Stupid.

Really stupid. Now I would do anything just to be stuck in Choirikell forever with Andy. If he were here, alive, I would never dream of anything else.

Helen realised Shelly was offering her a fresh candle on a plate. She took it and set it on the table next to her dying stub. Helen enjoyed watching the flickering flame. The dancing shadows cast across the table's knobbly surface soothed her. Maybe it was because Andy would have liked them too. He had seen the wonder in everything.

"How ye coping, Hel?"

Helen nearly replied, "*How the fuck d'ye think I'm coping?*" but she stopped herself. Shelly meant no harm; she was just trying to be kind. "I'm okay, Shell. Getting cold, though, so I might go upstairs and grab a wee nap."

Shelly rubbed at her shoulders and shivered. "I might join ye. Ye know, every time I close ma eyes, I picture waking up to a big muscly man in uniform."

"Like who? A soldier?"

"Nae, a fireman. I know it nae makes sense, but hey, I'm a sucker for a fireman."

Helen chuckled, but it was by rote rather than feeling. Shelly's smiling face was too much to bear, so she concentrated on the candle's flickering shadow. The living darkness. The darkness she prayed would soon take her.

Shelly sat at the table opposite Helen, something neither invited nor welcomed. "Must be a hundred of those disgusting things out there now. I keep seeing the faces of people we know, but it's nae them any more, right? I mean, they cannae still be in there."

"I've nae idea, Shell."

"Suppose none of us can know, really. Makes ye think, though, don't it? If we get infected, do ye think we'll feel ourselves slipping away? Like, will we stay trapped in the back of our brains while something takes control of our bodies? D'ye think it's like having a fever?"

"I dinnae know, Shell."

"D'ye think it hurts?"

"For feck sake, Shell, I dinnae know, all right? Go ask someone else."

Shelly flinched, then hopped up out of her chair and scurried away like a child trying to hold in tears.

Helen half rose to go after her. "Shell? Look, I'm sorry. Shell...? Ah, screw it!"

Helen dropped back down on her chair, deciding she didn't much care. Ed and Oliver glanced her way but quickly went back to minding their own business. Dale, however, came hurrying over. "Ye all right, Petal? What's the matter?"

"I'm fine. I just wanna be left alone."

"Aye, but I need to know yer all right. Dinnae give a feck aboot the rest of these gobshites, but ye'll always be ma lass, won't ye?"

"I'm not ye lass, Dale. I never will be again." Her defiance only made him smirk. He had always liked it when she fought back – enjoyed breaking her. Now that her life depended on staying inside his pub, he was getting possessive again. This time, there would be no one around to help her. The person who had helped her last time was probably dead.

How could she have turned her back on Miles?

How could she have not let him back inside the pub when he had begged? How could she have thrown that glass?

Because I was angry, and all I could see was my dead boy.

I owe Miles so much, but I turned my back on him. I chose Dale, just like I always used to. I deserve everything I get.

I've already lost everything.

Daffodil.

Dale put a hand on Helen's knee and leant in to whisper. "I'm gunna get us through this, ma wee petal. Then I'll find that English bastard and slice his neck like a fat goose. After that, we can try again. Ye'll always be ma lass, Hel. This time, things will be different. Better."

The world is over, Helen told herself, *and Dale might be the only thing standing between me and death. But do I even* want *to live?*

No.

Helen gave Dale a smile that lasted only as long as it took for him to leave. She watched him return to the bar and resume ordering around poor Ed. She saw the fear in Oliver's eyes as he tried to avoid Dale's attention.

The world was full of monsters.

IT'D BEEN over an hour since they'd returned to the women's tent. As a group, they'd become proficient at filling time, so everyone had occupied themselves in various ways while they waited for whatever happened next. Cameron was on his back, snoring. Aaron had his head buried in a car magazine. Ryan was perched on the edge of Fiona's bed, worrying and wondering. Were Sophie and his mam okay? Would he ever see them again?

Manchester was allegedly free of infection, but so had the army's camp been until an hour ago. The thought of never seeing

Sophie again – never kissing her or holding her – made him angry. He wanted to yell and throw a fit. He wanted to reach out across the universe and claw his way back to her, but the truth was that he was utterly powerless to do a single thing. Gradually, he worked himself up into such a state that he was glad when Lieutenant Holloway entered the tent and greeted them.

"How are things here?" the officer asked. He had his pistol out again, but thankfully it was aimed at the ground. His shirt was once again buttoned to the top, and he was wearing a black military beret. Had tonight been a wake-up call for him? Had Major Reid given him a dressing down?

"We're okay," said Miles. His eye patch had turned grubby and he itched at it every few minutes. Doctor Gerard would need to change the dressing soon. "What exactly happened out there?"

Holloway sighed. "A fuck-up, that's what. Several men were infected and failed to report it."

"Feckin' eejits," said Cameron. "Coulda killed the lot of us."

"Quite right," said Holloway, "except Doctor Gerard has a theory that they're not to blame."

Ryan inched forward on his cot bed. He was chilly, so he pulled a blanket over his lap. "Why not?"

Holloway gave a quick shrug. "Gerard thinks something about the fungus keeps its victims calm; prevents them from panicking and seeking help."

Aaron nodded. "Our friend Sean wasn't himself after he got infected. He didn't seem to realise how much trouble he was in."

Tom huffed at the rear of the tent. "Of course, it had nothing to do with all the drugs and alcohol in his system."

"Shut up," said Ryan, but he kept his focus on Holloway. "So people could be infected and not even know it? They wouldn't own up?"

"It appears that way. I'm going to have everyone checked twice a day from now on, including yourselves. It'll mean stripping down, I'm afraid."

"If I do that," said Cameron, glancing towards his crotch, "it'll knock the confidence of yer men. I can't even imagine what it'll do to the women."

Holloway rolled his eyes. "I'll risk it. Do any of you have any firearm experience?"

Everyone frowned. Even Cameron appeared confused, yet it was he who answered. "I used to go on the odd hunt wi' me da as a kid, and Dale Finley has shooting parties up on the hills twice a year. I've been to a few."

"Anyone else?" asked Holloway, and when nobody answered he grunted in displeasure. "I really hope I don't regret this." He held the pistol by the barrel and handed it grip-first it to Cameron. It was a modern style, with a clip instead of a revolving barrel. "You do not pull the trigger unless it's to take down a threat to camp. If I find out you pulled it for any other reason, I'll execute you on the spot. Got it?"

Cameron's mouth was hanging wide open as if he thought it some kind of prank. "W-Why are ye giving this to me?"

"Not you, specifically. I am giving it to your group. Vigilance is now vital. If you see a Kermit, put it down immediately. I won't have any more outbreaks in my camp."

"You mean Major Reid's camp?" said Aaron.

Holloway turned to face him. "What?"

Aaron shrunk back a little. "Isn't this Major Reid's camp?"

"Major Reid is very busy, but if you want to be pedantic, then, yes, he is the one in charge."

"Why hasn't he come to see us?" asked Cameron.

"Because he has bigger things to worry about."

Chloe was shaking her head, seeming in a world of her own. "How did those men get infected?"

It was a good question, so Ryan echoed it. "Yeah, you said they were infected, but how?"

Holloway folded his arms and sighed. It seemed all the man did lately was sigh. "Last night, three guards were attacked during a patrol," he said. "They were likely infected then."

"There were more than three," said Fiona. "I saw half a dozen. At least."

"Nine," said Holloway flatly. "We lost nine men. Not to mention the six who were injured during the attack. It's unlikely they'll remain healthy."

Cameron cursed. "Poor sods."

Holloway nodded, then turned to Miles. "Perhaps you could give them a blessing later tonight, Vicar? I would appreciate it."

"Whatever I can do, Lieutenant."

"Thank you."

"How were the other six men infected?" asked Ryan, not wanting to leave the mystery unexplained. "You only explained three."

"We believe it may have been rats."

Everyone gasped.

"Rats?" said Miles. "How?"

"There were several rat sightings during the night," said Holloway. "The men killed several, and the corpses were covered in fungus. Gerard assumes several men were bitten in their sleep. It only adds to his reasoning that they may have been unaware they were infected."

Everyone instinctively lifted their feet up onto the cot beds. Chloe whimpered. "How do we keep them out?"

Holloway put up a hand. "Just stay calm. Zip your tents up at night and you'll be fine. The canvas is strong enough to keep out rodents, and you have the pistol in case you spot anything."

Ryan exhaled through his nostrils, realising why the lieutenant had armed them. "It wasn't just infected *people* you were telling us to shoot, was it?"

"No. You see anything with the merest hint of green, you shoot it dead. Gerard will be by first thing every morning from now on to examine you for bites and scratches. You may stay together in this tent if it'll make your feel more secure."

Everyone was pleased to hear that, but something still

continued to nag at Ryan. "What about the other tent? The one with the old women and children?"

"I'm posting guards outside all civilian tents, so don't worry about them. You'll be safe so long as you stay calm and keep your eyes open. What happened tonight was a learning experience, but every lesson learned is a step closer to understanding and overcoming our enemy. This will not happen again."

"Of course not," said Cameron, but he didn't appear to mean it.

"You be careful with that pistol," warned Holloway. "Disrespect it and it's prone to go off in your face."

With that, the officer left them alone. Chloe rushed to zip up the tent flap behind him, and then everyone clambered into the middle of their cots. Getting to sleep that night was harder than ever.

4

R yan opened his eyes and sat up on his cot bed. There had been the odd spattering of rifle fire during the night, but daylight had arrived with little fanfare. The usual chitter-chatter and morning exercise drills had not yet begun in earnest. Was the camp still asleep?

Cameron got out of the adjacent cot bed, balls and penis dangling freely. The fact he was holding Holloway's pistol in his hand made him look deranged. Ryan shielded his eyes and yelled. "Fookin' 'ell, Cam, can you put on some keks?"

"What's the point? Gerard's coming by to strip-search us."

"Yeah, well, until then, put yourself away, man, before an infected rat comes and bites it off."

"Did you see any in the night?"

Ryan shook his head. "Of course not. I would have raised hell."

Fiona opened her eyes and rolled over. When she saw Cameron naked, she groaned. "Jesus, it looks like something crawled out of Chernobyl."

Chloe woke up and screamed.

Cameron smirked. "All right, ye jessies! I'll put some clothes on, but there's nowt wrong with the human body."

Ryan covered his eyes. "Just stop pointing that thing at me and get dressed."

Everyone awoke gradually, swigging from water bottles and munching on breakfast bars. A Portaloo sat outside the tent along with a pump-operated shower, but everyone was reluctant to leave the tent. Last night had been bad.

Tom stretched his arms and checked his watch. The expensive timepiece had a cracked face, and it clearly upset him every time he looked at it. It had been passed to him by his grandfather, a kindly old man Ryan had met a few times back when he and Tom were kids. "It's almost ten past seven. Did anyone hear the bell?"

Fiona shook her head. "It would've woken us."

Chloe stifled a yawn, then said, "Maybe everyone's getting a lie-in. Last night was pretty intense."

It was plausible, and no one had any other suggestions.

"Anyone see any rats in the night?" asked Aaron.

"No," said Tom. He cupped a hand to his bandaged earlobe and winced. "I slept quite well actually."

Chloe yawned again. "Not me. I nae slept a wink. Kept hearing wee scratching feet. Rats freak me out."

"Everything freaks you out," said Cameron. He was dressed now, and he tucked Holloway's pistol into the waistband of his trousers before covering it with his jumper.

"Not true. I like snakes."

Aaron frowned. "Snakes?"

Chloe nodded. "Yeah. I held a wee corn snake at the zoo once and have loved them ever since. If we had a few snakes around the place, we would nae need to worry aboot rats."

"Good point."

"My Amanda likes snakes, too," said Tom. "Last month I took her to Chester Zoo, and I could barely drag her away from the terrariums."

Chloe smiled. "I hope I get to meet her then."

Tom nodded. "Yes, I hope so too. That would be nice. It's still early days in our relationship, but I have high hopes. Yes, high hopes indeed."

Ryan decided to get the ball rolling on the toilet breaks. His bladder was full to bursting, and he'd always had a weird phobia that holding it could cause damage. "I'll go check things out. I'm sure everything is fine."

Everyone nodded, but no one offered to join him. There was an unaddressed fear in the room, and Ryan had just volunteered to face it on behalf of the group.

Relief was the first thing he felt when he exited the tent. The camp hadn't burned down during the night or become overrun with greens. Soldiers rushed back and forth busily as normal, while others ate from mess tins or exercised in open spaces. Every now and then, an old truck would depart the camp. A dozen of the rusty old vehicles sat parked in a line at the camp's rear edge. Seeing them driving back and forth was the only hint that there was still a civilisation left out there. Ryan didn't know why these particular vehicles still drove, but Aaron had tried to explain that it was something to do with EMP only affecting newer vehicles.

Holloway stood at the rear of the camp, outside the command tent, giving orders. Things were under control.

All the same, Ryan was unsettled as he headed to the Portaloo. Something felt off. In fact, he had a hard time peeing because of how anxious he felt. They didn't receive a single update during the night, and no expected summons for Miles came either. There had been no visits from Dr Gerard. Pure exhaustion had eventually sent them all to sleep.

After Ryan finished peeing, he stepped back out into camp and finally realised what was wrong, yet he didn't necessarily understand it. His anxiety sent him hurrying back inside the tent, where shared he his concerns with the others.

Cameron stuck his head out of the flap, then turned back inside. "English is right. Half the camp's missing."

Everyone took turns peering out through the gap. The verdict was universal – half the soldiers and other personnel had disappeared. The camp was partially deserted.

"What does it mean?" asked Chloe. She was running her fingers through her blonde and pink hair, trying to pull out the knots and retie a ponytail. Her eyes were once again dark, but with tiredness now instead of make-up.

Miles shrugged. "Perhaps they went into the village, finally, to look for survivors."

"We would've heard them," said Aaron. "If a hundred soldiers suddenly armed up and headed out into the night, we would've known about it. Not to mention it would be a lot smarter to launch a mission during daylight."

Tom nodded. "I'm inclined to agree. The dark would be a hindrance against the greens. I don't think it's possible to catch them sleeping."

Ryan wrung his hands together. "What then? Where did half the camp suddenly go?"

"One way to find out," said Cameron, lifting the tent flap. "I'm gunna go see Major Reid. I wanna know why he's stopped showing his face around here."

Fiona shook her head. "He's going to get us all shot."

Miles yelled after him. "Cameron Pollock, yoo get back here at once! We'll have nae trouble today, thank yoo very much."

"Bollocks! I'm going."

Cameron disappeared through the flap and Ryan hurried after him as usual, resigned to forever becoming involved in the big Scot's shenanigans. He was glad when he heard everyone else following.

They were abruptly brought to a halt by the same corporal who had obstructed them the previous night when they had been trying to move across camp – Corporal Kay. He was standing with the beanie-hatted private who had jumped up to help him after Cameron had bust his nose. The way the two men glared at Cameron was murderous.

Kay's nose was cut across the bridge and dark bruises

stained his eye sockets. The scar on his cheek was bright pink with the cold. "Camp's in lockdown," he growled. "Back in yer tents!"

"We're allowed to roam," said Miles. "What do ye mean, *lockdown*?"

The corporal looked ready for round two with Cameron, but there was a nervous, bird-like quality to his movements. He seemed to find it hard to keep his eyes focused on one place. "The camp. Is. In. Lockdown," he repeated. "All non-military personnel are to remain inside their tents."

"Aye," said Beanie Hat, pointing his rifle. "Dinnae make us ask again."

"Where is everyone?" asked Ryan, softly so as not to agitate the soldiers further. "Dr Gerard hasn't been by. The morning bell didn't ring either."

"Get back in yer tent," Beanie Hat growled.

"Make us," said Cameron, stepping forward. Thankfully, he didn't reveal the pistol beneath his jumper.

Miles put a hand against his puffed-out chest. "There will be nae violence."

"Back in yer tent," Corporal Kay demanded, "or there will be." He glared at Cameron, shaking hands bunched into fists.

Chloe stepped to the front of the group and batted her eyelids at the corporal. "We're just scared. None of us have been able to get any sleep. Those poor men, last night, who were infected... Were they friends of yours?"

Kay relaxed a little, anger filtering away slightly. His fists loosened. "Aye, every one of them. Look, I cannae tell ye anything, all right?"

"Too right," said Beanie Hat. "Yer all lucky to still be suckin' breath after what ye did."

"To be fair," said Tom. "That was Cameron."

"Thanks for the backup, Poshie."

"You're welcome."

"I've spent ma entire life in Choirikell," said Chloe. "Everyone

I care about is in the village. Please, we just want to know what's happening."

"Please. Go back in yer tents."

"Or I'll drag ye there," said Beanie Hat.

Cameron sneered.

Kay closed his eyes and took a few deep breaths. He placed a hand on Beanie Hat's rifle and lowered it. "Dan, just give me a minute, eh? I'll be right along."

Beanie Hat – or *Dan* – curled his lip. "What ye talking aboot, pal? Let's teach these wee shites a lesson."

Corporal Kay's expression turned grim. His blackened eyes made him look like a ghoul. "Just give me a wee minute, eh? Holloway will have ma bollocks if another scrap breaks out, so just leave it oot, eh? I'll be right with ye, Dan, all right?"

Dan was clearly disgruntled. He glared at Cameron and slowly backed away, before finally turning and stomping his way across camp.

Corporal Kay rubbed at his forehead and blew air out of his cheeks. "Are yoo lot gunna cause me problems, because I have to say I've enough to do around here?"

"We're not looking for trouble," said Fiona.

"Well, *most* of us aren't," said Tom, rolling his eyes.

Chloe took another step closer to the corporal. She spoke quietly, conspiratorially. "Something's happened, hasn't it? Where has everybody gone? Please, we just need someone to be on our side for a minute."

"Ye really need to get back inside yer tents," said Kay. His demeanour was concerned now instead of combative. "It's dangerous oot here."

"We just need to know what's happening. Where has everybody gone?"

Kay glanced left and right, swallowed, then appeared to deflate like a perishing balloon. "Ah fine, who gives a shit, anyway? Everything is shagged, all right? Last night, we screened the camp fer infection and found eighteen cases.

Holloway ordered the poor bastards shot right there and then."
He looked away, might even have been fighting back tears. "We
feckin' shot our own men. After that, half the camp went
AWOL in the night. Wish I'd gone with 'em. This is the end
times."

Miles did the sign of the cross. "May God save us."

Corporal Kay snarled. "God has nowt to do with this."

Cameron folded his thick arms. "Where the feck is Major
Reid in all this?"

Kay clearly retained his dislike of Cameron, but he obviously
decided to let his grudges die because he gave an answer,
although it contained a fine helping of scorn. "Major Reid? Major
Reid topped himself three days ago, pal. Holloway's been tryna
keep the CO's death on the quiet. Last thing we need is an
outbreak of morphine overdoses and whisky binges."

Ryan nodded. It made sense. "Holloway's worried the news
will demoralise everyone."

"Aye. Morale is as vital to an army as good scran and thick
boots. That horse has bolted now, though."

"What do you mean?" asked Tom. "You still have enough
soldiers to keep things under control here, right?"

"Keep *what* under control? It's all fecked."

Cameron grabbed the corporal's arm. "What are ye saying?"

Kay shrugged free of Cameron's grasp and grew angry. "Figure
it oot for yerselves, eh? Just... Just stay oot of ma way. I ain't
forgotten last night." He turned and stormed off, muttering to
himself like a madman.

"Well, that wasn't comforting," said Fiona. "He looks ready to
have a nervous breakdown."

"Can ye blame him?" said Chloe. "Poor guy."

Ryan shrugged. "At least we learned something. Good work,
getting him to open up like that, Chloe. I thought you liked
women, though."

"I do. Obviously so does he."

Fiona was shaking her head, barely listening. "I can't believe

Major Reid committed suicide. Why would he do that when so many people were relying on him?"

"Because he knew how bad things were," said Aaron. "He knew better than anyone, and he decided killing himself was better than facing whatever's coming next. Maybe it really is the end times."

Miles argued. "We don't know why he killed himself, so let's not jump to conclusions."

"He must've thought things were pretty hopeless," said Fiona. "Or else he wouldn't have chosen suicide."

"Nothing is hopeless," said Miles, "so long as we believe in ourselves."

Cameron patted Miles on the back. "That's lovely, Vicar, but I dinnae think it's true. Come on. Let's go speak to Holloway."

"Wait," said Tom, "is that a good idea? He shot a dozen of his own men last night."

"He hadnae any choice," said Cameron. "They were infected. I woulda done the same. Didn't ye learn yer lesson after Stewart and Gavin?"

"I'm just saying that it doesn't sound like he has a lot of patience left. We should go back inside our tent and wait for everything to settle down."

"Sod that!" Cameron started marching. "I've had enough of freezing ma balls off in a fart-filled bag. I'm heading for the hills. Maybe I'll camp out on ma own."

"Foolish," said Miles. "We're better off together."

"And the farts all belong to you," said Aaron.

"Well, I dinnae plan on heading doon across the border with the rest o' ye, so where does that leave me? One way or another, I'm gunna end up on ma own, same as always."

Chloe hugged herself, shivering against the cold. "We should stay together. All of us."

"Let's just talk to Holloway," said Ryan. "See what's what before we think any further ahead."

"Aye," said Cameron, "but this ends today, one way or

another. No more being kept prisoner while the world goes to pot."

Everybody looked at one another, but no one argued. As frightening as things were, the dread of spending another day inside an empty tent made taking a risk seem a little more palatable. Ryan, for one, was desperate to get home, no matter the cost.

Before home disappears.

Holloway was still standing outside the command tent, but instead of giving orders, he was now looking over a bundle of papers. When he saw Cameron and the others approaching, he groaned. "What are you all doing, walking around?"

"Just stretching our legs," said Miles. "Ye said we were allowed to wander."

"That was before the events of last night. You should all go back to your tents."

"Last we checked," said Cameron, "we were human beings, not guinea pigs. We're done being ye pets."

Miles winced. "What he means to say is, we need some fresh air."

Holloway let it go. He looked tired, under strain. "Fine, just don't get in anybody's way, least of all mine."

"Where's Dr Gerard?" Miles pointed at his bandaged eye, then adjusted the loose bandages around his head. "I need to have ma dressings changed. Painkillers wouldn't go amiss either."

"Dr Gerard is busy. I'll have a medic come by and see to you shortly."

Miles nodded, but Cameron tutted. "Gerard go AWOL with the rest of 'em, did he? Right after ye shot yer own men? Or maybe he decided to follow Major Reid's lead and topped himself."

Everyone cringed.

"Jesus, Cameron," said Ryan.

Holloway was clearly taken by surprise because he flinched,

but then he grew angry, red in the face and upper lip curling. "Where have you been getting your information?"

Cameron shrugged. "Word gets around, pal."

"Is it true?" asked Ryan, deciding he probably couldn't piss off the lieutenant any more than Cameron already had. "Is Dr Gerard one of the men who left?"

Holloway snorted, his anger exhaling as though he were too weak to hold it. "He had some unsettling news. I assume he's halfway to Aberdeen by now."

Tom frowned. "What bad news?"

"That would be the doctor's business, now, wouldn't it?"

"I wasn't intending to be nosey. I was merely asking out of concern, Lieutenant."

Holloway gave a small shrug. "It concerns his family, let's leave it at that."

"You mean the family he has in York?"

"Perhaps." He sniffed. "Did any of you spot rats in the night? I trust not?"

"No," said Miles. "Did anyone else?"

"A few were spotted, but nothing that couldn't be handled."

Ryan rubbed at his face, trying to put some warmth in his cheeks. Despite eating well, the broken sleep and multiple healing wounds were exacerbating his exhaustion. "Just level with us, Lieutenant. Things have clearly turned bad around here, so where's the harm in us knowing the score? We may even be able to help."

"I doubt it. Look, you really want to know the truth? You think you're hard done by, sitting around here safe and sound inside a tent with food in your bellies and guards outside? The *truth* is that half my men abandoned their posts in the night, and no one will be coming to replace them. All remaining forces have been recalled to Edinburgh to protect the capital and the Scottish border. We have orders to desert this hill ASAP." He cleared his throat and looked away. "Things are growing increasingly challenging."

Ryan didn't like the officer's defeated tone. "Is Manchester still okay? Is it?"

Holloway tossed his stack of papers at the muddy ground as though they had never been of any interest in the first place. Ryan glanced at one of the sheets and saw rows upon rows of hand-writing and drawings. Orders from somewhere.

"Our messengers returned from Liverpool at five this morn-ing," said Holloway. "The infection has broken out in the buffer zone, and anyone healthy is being evacuated across the Scottish border. We're going to concentrate our remaining resources there and try to hold a line. Maybe if we can maintain a barrier... I don't know. Anyway, it's all we have. In the meantime, I have received orders to burn Choirikell to the ground. We don't have the resources to maintain two borders, so we need to make sure the fungus doesn't spread from here southwards."

Ryan felt woozy. He lost his footing and put out an arm, but he failed to grab hold of anything to break his fall. He ended up on his knees in the mud. Aaron crouched beside him and held him as if he were the older of the two. "Hey, it's gunna be all right, man. I'm here."

"We need to get home, Aaron. We need to go get Mam and Sophie, and take them some place safe."

Holloway knelt beside the two brothers, forming a huddle. He looked ready to lie down and go to sleep, but his expression was compassionate, if impatient. Difficult to imagine him shooting eighteen of his own men mere hours ago. "We'll be heading south at sunrise tomorrow," he told them. "It'll take a little time to get packed up here, so there's time to get some rest. You should try and sleep."

"What if people are still alive in Choirikell?" asked Fiona.

Holloway stood back up. "There's no *if* about it, but that doesn't change what needs to be done."

Miles frowned. "There are survivors in the village? You've confirmed it?"

"We took a woman in a few nights ago. She was badly

wounded, so she's resting in the infirmary, but before she fell unconscious, she told us about people hiding inside the village pub." He turned to Miles. "Probably the same people who tossed a glass at your face. I would love to see them safe, but I won't throw my men to the lions."

Miles nodded thoughtfully. "They've remained safe this whole time. Good for them."

Fiona folded her arms and looked back across camp, towards Choirikell. "We need to warn them. Who knows how many people are still alive?"

Holloway shook his head, blinking slowly. "I won't risk my remaining men – they're too precious. The people at the pub are likely dead or infected by now, and if not, the burden lies on them to save *themselves*. We're burning this place to the ground come morning. Just be thankful you made it out."

Chloe covered her mouth in horror. "How can ye burn a bunch of innocent people alive?"

"The same way I shot my own men," said Holloway, showing no sign of shame. "It needed to be done. This is about the big ugly picture now, my friends. We must contain this fungus at any cost. Any *human* cost. Don't force me to teach you that lesson personally, because I will not hesitate. You wanted the truth, well, there it is."

Miles groaned. "Ye've made yerself abundantly clear, Lieutenant. Thank you."

"Stay the night or leave today, it's up to you. I don't much care."

Holloway marched away, already barking orders to anyone unlucky enough to get caught in his path. One of the bonfires had already been dismantled, and several tents lay flattened. The camp was disappearing piece by piece.

Miles reached down and helped Ryan to his feet. Aaron grabbed him under the armpits to keep him upright. It was Cameron who spoke. "Looks like I'm heading south after all."

RYAN'S HAND WAS SHAKING. The large gash on his forearm, caused by tumbling over a barbed wire fence several days ago, throbbed painfully. No medic had visited the tent as promised, and Dr Gerard was clearly long gone. They all had bandages that needed changing.

For the last twenty minutes, Ryan and his companions had been sitting on their cot beds in near silence, probably all thinking the same thing – that this was the end of the world. Corkscrews had fallen from the skies and unleashed an alien fungus upon the Earth and all life was slowly being consumed and corrupted. It wasn't a tragedy unique to Ryan, as he had assumed back at the cottage when Sean and Brett had died. Back then, he had pictured police interviews and news reporters asking how he had heroically survived such an ordeal. Instead, he had discovered his plight to be a mere footnote on a worldwide catastrophe. Less than a footnote. An errant comma.

And we all thought global warming was what would kill us.

"There's no end to this, is there?" said Chloe, her legs crossed atop her mattress. She plucked at the thinning black jean fabric around her knees, yanking at the delicate white threads within. "Part of me just wants to go home. I mean, my house is right there up the hill. Ma is probably wandering around like everybody else, but she could be hiding in her bedroom, safe and sound. She could be okay."

"Shit," said Ryan. "I never even thought about it. You have family in the village?"

Chloe nodded. Her expression was firm, like she was forcing herself to be strong. "Only me ma. Ma dad left when I was twelve. He works at a prison in Glasgow. I see him a few times a year. Maybe he's doing okay too."

"Yeah, maybe." Ryan turned his head. "What about you, Miles? Have you got family in the village?"

Miles shook his head, a loose flap of bandage swishing back

and forth. "Lifelong bachelor, me. Plenty of friends, though. I've been hoping this thing would eventually blow over, that everyone in the village would be okay, but I suppose it's time to stop kidding myself. I pray for the poor souls of Choirikell."

"Me ma died last year of the cancer," said Cameron, scratching at the coppery hairs emerging from his cheeks. "Kind of glad aboot it now."

"I'm sorry," said Ryan.

Cameron nodded, and for once he had no blustery reply. In fact, it was clear, in that moment, that the big, manly Scot had loved his mother very much. Somehow, it made him a great deal more tolerable.

"We all have family," said Tom. "It's probably the one thing we've got in common."

Ryan huffed. "You and I used to have a lot more in common than that. It's like I don't even know you any more, man."

Tom said nothing for a moment, he just stared at Ryan. Eventually, he spoke. "I know this situation has come between us, Ryan, but I don't see any point in apportioning blame. We're each dealing with things in the best way we see fit."

"But you're the only one who's been an arse about it," said Aaron.

Everyone chuckled. Funnily enough, so did Tom. "Perhaps," he admitted. "I regret being at odds with you these last few days, Ryan. It's not what I would've hoped for."

"Me either," said Ryan, and he chided himself for it. He wanted to stay mad at Tom, and once again, he spitefully wished that Loobey were the one who was still alive. Loobey would never have turned his back on Ryan and Aaron like Tom had back at the bowls club. Loobey had been a loyal friend right up until the very end.

Right until that thing absorbed him.

Tom sighed. "Well, perhaps we can fix things somewhere down the line. Right now, I'm tired and afraid, and I want to get home to see the people I care about."

"There are supposed to be people *here* that you care about, man."

Miles put a hand up, glancing between them both with his one good eye. "Let's try to keep on the same page. We're lucky to have found one another in this crisis. It was meant to be."

Cameron farted. "Anyone fancy ham?"

Everyone laughed.

"What about the people in the pub?" asked Chloe, growing serious, like the laughter had somehow shamed her. "They're probably people we know. Neighbours. We can't let them burn to death. We need to warn them."

"I agree," said Miles. "In fact, I've already decided I'm heading back into the village."

"Yer mad," said Cameron. He looked horrified.

"I am perfectly sane, thank ye very much, Cameron Pollock. I am also Choirikell's chaplain. How can I look maself in the eye if I'm willing to leave friends and neighbours to die? I dinnae have a choice in this."

"I'm coming with ye," said Chloe. She reached into her pocket and pulled out a fluffy pink keyring and some keys. "I want to go home. I want to get some of ma things before they're gone forever."

"Ye cannae risk yer life for trinkets, lass."

"I'm not. I'm risking my life to help the people still alive in the village. Me ma could be one of them."

Miles nodded thoughtfully. "Then I'll be glad to have ye along, Chloe."

"I'm going, too," said Aaron, holding a rolled-up magazine in his hand. He batted it against his palm to make his point.

Ryan gasped. "Aaron, you can't—"

Aaron shook the magazine at him like an angry finger. "Don't try to change my mind, Ryan. Last week, I was just this weird and lonely kid – I probably still am – but now I'm surrounded by people who have risked their necks for me. If I don't do the same for them, then what's the point, huh? Why try to survive if we leave others to die?"

Fiona moved away from her cot bed and gave Aaron a friendly punch on the arm. "Friends who fight monsters together—"

"Die together," said Tom, rolling his eyes. "You don't even know for sure that there's anyone left alive to warn. Holloway said himself that his intel is a couple of days old."

Ryan exhaled, terrified at the mere thought of re-entering the village of the damned. "This is insane. I need to keep you safe, Aaron."

"I understand that, but if there's any hope of getting back home, we're going to need help. And to get help, you have to give it. Besides, you torched a load of greens when you set fire to Miles's church. Not to mention those the army dealt with. How many can there be left? We'll be fine."

"Then, I suppose I'm in." Ryan shook his head, barely believing what he'd just agreed to.

"Feckin' 'ell," said Cameron. "Whoever thought I'd be rushing into a fight with a bunch of English at ma side?"

Ryan chuckled. "Well, it *did* take the end of the world for it to happen."

"Aye, it did."

A silence descended, and slowly, one by one, everyone looked at Tom.

Tom grunted. "What? You want me to risk my life to help a group of people I've never met? *Thugs*, no less. They almost blinded you, Miles, or did you forget?"

Miles shrugged. "Accidents happen."

"This would be a good way to start repairing our friendship," said Ryan. "Might be a laugh, mate. We can tell Sophie and Amanda all about it once we get home. Maybe watch a movie afterwards. A good one. One without any superheroes in it. Come on, what's the worst that can happen. I mean, a lot, of course, but maybe it will all be okay."

"Can you please stop talking?" Tom folded his arms, exhaled, then spluttered. "Fine, but I wish to register my complete dissatisfaction at this plan."

"Noted. Thanks, mate."

"Aye," said Cameron. "I was wondering how long it would take fer ye to grow some bollocks."

"Don't talk to me about bollocks, Cameron, because I've seen more than enough of yours."

Cameron's upper lip quivered, his eyes narrowed, then he cracked a smile. "Aye, guilty as charged there, Poshie."

"So when do we do this?" asked Aaron.

"Now," said Fiona. "Who knows how long it'll be before Holloway starts setting fires? Not to mention we won't have much daylight if we don't do this soon."

"I don't fancy risking my life in the dark," said Tom. "I prefer to see the things trying to eat me."

"They're not zombies," said Aaron. "Worst they'll do is slice your face open with their talons and turn you into one of them."

Tom folded his arms and grimaced. "I stand corrected. Can I just restate, for the record, that we have no idea if we will even find anyone alive in the village to warn? This could be a fool's errand. In fact, it's likely to be."

Miles fiddled with his eye dressing, itching at it gently. "We all heard Holloway say there was a survivor in the infirmary. Someone who saw the people at the pub a couple of days ago. Perhaps we should pay this person a visit."

Tom winced. "Entering an infirmary during a quarantine does not seem wise. What if this woman is infectious?"

"Then Holloway would have shot her like he did his own men," said Aaron. "No, she must have injured herself some other way."

Fiona was nodding. "It would be good to know as much as possible about what we're heading into. Even you must agree with that, Tom?"

"I suppose I do. If we're set upon running around like

commandos, we should probably get the most up-to-date intel we can – even if it is two days old."

"*Manc* commandos," said Ryan, looking at Fiona and winking.

Tom frowned. "What?"

He shook his head. "Never mind. So, are we all in agreement then, about sneaking into the infirmary before heading into the village?"

Everybody nodded.

"Great," said Cameron. "I'm just gunna go take a dump, then we can head oot and make some feckin' mischief."

ED COULD BARELY KEEP QUIET. The terror on the young lad's face was so white hot it looked set to burst his eyeballs. Helen had to grab him and move him away from the window before he became hysterical. She shushed him and forced him to look at her. "Keep yer mouth shut. If that thing hears us, we're finished. Do you understand me?"

Ed's eyelids were barely visible, stretched so wide. The thing outside frightened everyone, but they all needed to keep their shit together. The army was close by – their gunfire was as regular as clockwork now, a faint voice kept calling out from somewhere – but the pub was surrounded and only getting more so. The only way to stay alive was by keeping quiet and staying put. She didn't know if the army was planning a rescue, but if it was, it needed to get a move on.

Once Helen was sure Ed wouldn't scream the house down, she moved back over to the window. There, Dale stood with his shotgun folded across his arm, clearly wondering whether to take a shot at the road below. Doing so would be a stupid idea in her opinion. Just staring out of the bedroom window was dangerous enough if that monstrous thing happened to glance upwards with its single giant eye.

Helen shuddered being so close to Dale. She didn't know if it was revulsion or attraction. "We should back away and stay quiet."

Dale nodded, but he didn't move away. "What is that thing? Ye told me this was some kind of fungus. What kind of fungus does that?"

Helen could give no answer. The thing in the road was the size of a minibus and growing larger every hour. It now moved on all fours, with a single giant eyeball buried in its shoulder. Several of the nearby greens seemed to be attached to the larger creature, their limbs slowly being enveloped by the central mass. Perhaps that's how the thing was growing – absorbing the bodies of Helen's former friends and neighbours. A dozen floating heads hung from its fibrous torso in various clusters, all of them open-mouthed and silently screaming. The abomination was covered in so much thick green fur that it appeared to shimmer.

"Dale, we cannae do anything. Let's just move away and wait for it to piss off."

"Wait for it to piss off? The thing's getting bigger by the minute. If we don't deal with it now, it'll smash right through this place."

"Only if it knows we're inside."

"Oh, it knows. Those greens have been surrounding the pub for days. They know we're in here. That's why we've been dealing with so many bugs."

Helen supposed it could be true. During the last few hours, they had been assaulted by dozens of fat little bugs coming in through the gaps beneath the main doors. Dale had stomped them all to mush and then blocked the gap with towels, but it had put everyone on edge. It felt like the enemy were starting to get in, and it could only be a matter of time before they tried again. Close to a hundred greens ambled around outside. They could storm the pub with no effort at all if they wanted to. So why weren't they?

Are they starving us out? Are they smart?

Maybe the big one is. It's not like the others. It's something else. It's...

Alien.

"We have to get oot o' here," said Dale, "before it's too late."

"It's *already* too late. We need to wait for the army to come and deal with this mess."

Dale looked at her in the way that always made her feel like a little girl. "Are ye fer real? Ain't no one coming for us, ma wee petal. The army's had nearly a week to come into the village, but they've done nowt but stay on the outside. Rescue ain't their mission."

"What do ye mean?"

"Yer've never seen the world fer what it is, have ye? The army has stayed outside the village this whole time. Why do ye think that is? It's to make sure nowt gets out. Our only chance at living is to get oot o' here and head for the hills. Ma family has a wee cabin in the south glen. Stocked full of supplies, it is. If we can get there, we can wait this thing oot."

"And what if there's no waiting it oot, Dale? What if this doesnae get any better?"

"Then a wee cabin in the middle of nowhere is probably our best bet, eh? We're getting oot of here, soon as I see a chance. Ma pub, ma rules."

Helen sighed. "Move away from the window then. If yer gunna get everyone killed, at least let them have some lunch first."

We're all going to die.

I can hardly wait.

I'm coming for you, Andy.

5

The infirmary was at the opposite end of camp, near the command tent where Holloway spent most of his time. A dozen soldiers were in the area, but none seemed particularly observant or interested in anything beyond what they were doing. Many appeared skittish, like Corporal Kay had been. None of them chatted or engaged in the usual horseplay. The atmosphere had changed.

Ryan had a plan. "Let's head to the command tent again. Anyone who sees us will assume we're going to talk to Holloway. Then a couple of us can sneak off to the infirmary."

"Okay," said Miles. "Sounds like a plan."

They headed across the camp in a huddle. Miles walked at the front because his dog collar summoned respectful nods from the soldiers instead of glares. Cameron remained at the rear for the opposite reason. A few moments later, they were outside the command tent. Luckily, Holloway was distracted, talking to a group of soldiers ten feet away with his back turned to them.

"Okay," said Miles quietly. "I'm pretty sure that's the infirmary over there. Who should go?"

"I will," said Ryan, wanting to be useful. The infirmary was a long white tent with no markings, but it was where Dr Gerard had spent a majority of his time before leaving.

"I'll go with you," said Aaron.

"Nah," said Chloe. "Neither of ye know anyone from the village. I'll go wi' him."

Aaron nodded, and so did Ryan. It made sense, so he and Chloe broke away from the group in a hurry. Their destination was ten metres away, with only a single guard posted. As expected, the soldier stopped them as soon as they got too close. "What are ye doin'?"

Chloe didn't allow Ryan time to speak. She walked up to the guard and, unbelievably, ran the exact same routine she had with Corporal Kay. "Hey, sorry to be bother ye, we nae want to cause a fuss, but we spoke with Holloway and he told us aboot someone ye brought into camp a couple nights ago."

The guard's eyes narrowed. He didn't speak.

Chloe carried on. "I'm worried it's ma auntie Val. She's the only family I got since a heart attack took away ma dad. I just... I have to know if it's her." She took a step closer to the guard, looking like she might burst into tears. "Please, help me."

The guard fidgeted uncomfortably and swallowed. "I... um, Holloway said it was okay, did he?"

Chloe nodded. "As long as we dinnae get in anybody's way, he said."

The guard nodded to the tent flap. "All right, go right ahead then."

Chloe touched the soldier on the arm and smiled. "Thank you. I'm Chloe, by the way."

"Steve."

"Thanks, Steve."

"Yer welcome."

Ryan entered the tent two steps behind Chloe. Chloe had a hand across her mouth, trying not to giggle. "So easy."

"Wow," said Ryan. "You should become a spy after all this is through. You can talk yourself out of anything."

"I was thinking more like an actress," she said, giggling quietly. "I've always dreamt of heading to London and trying to make it on TV. If not for me ma, I probably would have left as soon as I turned sixteen."

"I suppose life must be pretty quiet living up here. Until recently."

"You have no idea."

"Well, if TV still exists, I definitely think you have a future."

"Thanks."

"I always wanted to take guitar lessons. I suppose, living in Manchester—"

Chloe shushed him. They'd made it into the tent's main section. There were three people sleeping and a dozen empty beds. Two of the snoozers were tough-looking men – probably soldiers – but at the rear of the tent was a middle-aged woman with a mass of tangled blonde hair on her pillow. The noises she made were not reassuring. Every breath sounded as if it might be her last.

"Oh God, it's Sam," said Chloe in a hushed voice.

"Who's Sam?"

"She runs a daycare at her house; looks after all the bairns. She's lovely. Come on, let's see if I can wake her up."

"Maybe you shouldn't. She's in bad shape."

"We cannae make her any worse, can we? We need to know what she saw."

"I suppose you're right. Okay, come on." Ryan moved along with Chloe, remaining a step behind to allow her to deal with things however she saw fit. She knew this woman, so she should be the one to lead.

Chloe placed a hand on the woman's bedcovers, locating the shape of her leg and shaking it gently. "Hey? Hey, Sam?"

It took a while, but slowly the woman roused. Her eyes peeled open and she glanced around, blinking rapidly, not seeming to understand where she was. Then her gaze settled on Chloe and she relaxed a little. "Chloe? Wh-Where am I? Are the children okay?"

"They're fine. Were yoo the one who got them here? How?"

The woman licked at her cracked lips, a fetid stench wafting from her mouth. "We-We were surrounded. I told the children to run. We made it most of the way, but... but there was a loud bang. Soldiers came. I-I don't remember anything else apart from the pain."

Chloe turned back to Ryan, a questioning look on her face. "Reckon they shot her?"

Ryan grimaced. "Nothing would surprise me at this point."

Sam tried to reach out, but her arm barely moved above the covers. "Th-The children?"

Chloe shushed her. "I promise, they're fine, Sam. You saved them. The soldiers must have fired before realising ye weren't one of the greens, but the bairns are okay."

"You're a hero," said Ryan softly.

Chloe nodded, but the woman didn't seem to care whether she was a hero or not. Chloe placed a hand against her cheek and smiled. "Sam? The army is getting everybody out of here in the morning, but anyone still in the village is going to get left behind. That's why I'm here. Sam, listen to me. Did ye see anyone still alive in the village? At the pub, maybe?"

Sam closed her eyes like she was going to go back to sleep, but she managed to answer. "Dale Finley. Others too. They were all... okay."

Chloe looked back at Ryan and grimaced. "Dale Finley is the local villain. I would nae risk my life fer the likes of him, but..."

Ryan nodded. "The others."

"They tried to help me," said Sam in a dreamy whisper. "They opened the doors."

"Okay," said Ryan. "So now we know for sure. We have to get to the pub and warn whoever's there."

Chloe turned back to Sam. "Hey, Sam, how come the people in the pub never left with yoo and the bairns?"

"Monster."

"A monster?" Chloe gave the woman a gentle shake. "What do you mean, Sam? What monster?" But the woman didn't reply. Her head flopped on the pillow and a thin line of blood-streaked drool trickled from her lips. Chloe shook her harder. "Sam? Sam, wake up. Wake up, Sam."

Ryan grabbed Chloe by the shoulders and eased her away. The conversation had clearly reached its end. Sam was still alive, but barely. The rising and falling of her chest was almost undetectable.

Chloe shook off Ryan's grasp, pulled back Sam's bedsheets, and then groaned. She covered her mouth. "Oh…"

Ryan swore.

Sam's torso was wrapped in bloodstained bandages that clearly hadn't been changed in a while. The stink coming off her was almost fruity.

Chloe snarled. "Dr Gerard abandoned her like this. That sonofabitch."

"Come on," said Ryan. "There's nothing we can do for her. We need to get back to the others."

"Aye."

They hurried out of the tent but didn't get past the guard. He grabbed Chloe by the arm. "Is it?"

Chloe shrugged out of his grasp, taken by surprise. "Is it *what*?"

"Is it yer auntie Val?"

"Oh. No, it's not her. It's someone else, but she needs help. She's dying in there."

The guard sighed. "There's nothing we can do. I'm sorry."

"Sorry? Ye could at least change her bandages."

Ryan dragged her away. "Come on, we need to get back to the others."

The guard looked genuinely upset by Chloe's outburst. He ducked beneath the flap and entered the tent, hopefully to go check on Samantha. Ryan feared the man was right, and that there really was nothing anyone could do.

Cameron and the others had remained outside the command tent, but Holloway was now speaking to them. He did not look happy. "Do I need to have you people shot?" he was asking, and when he noticed Ryan and Chloe coming from the direction of the infirmary, he turned and said, "and where exactly have you been?"

"I, um…" Ryan waited for Chloe to do her thing, but she stayed quiet.

"Ye said ye'd send a medic," said Miles, rescuing the situation. "We need pain relief. Ryan has a missing toe and my eye is throbbing like a teenager's cock."

Tom pointed to his bandaged earlobe. "This also hurts much more than one would think."

"I have a tummy ache," said Aaron.

Ryan nodded. "Yeah, um, Chloe and I went to the infirmary hoping to find somebody. We're all suffering."

Holloway grew less angry. "Yes, okay, fine. Let me grab someone for you." He peered around the camp, a hand over his eyes to shield them from the sun. After a moment, he let out a high-pitched whistle that caused everyone to turn his way. Clicking his fingers, he put an arm in the air. "Sergeant White! Get over here."

A woman in her mid-to-late twenties came rushing over from the centre of the camp. She stamped to a halt in front of Holloway and gave a salute. "Yessir?"

"These civilians are in need of pain relief. Can you find whatever Gerard didn't steal and dispense it accordingly?"

"Of course, sir. Right away, sir." The soldier turned to Ryan and the others with a smile, which was probably the first one they'd got from anyone at the camp since arriving. "Go rest in your tent, folks. I'll be by as soon as I can."

Miles nodded. "Most appreciated."

Ryan started walking back towards the tent. The others joined him. Miles moved up beside Chloe and whispered. "Did ye find anything?"

"Aye," said Chloe. "There are definitely people at the pub."

"And a monster apparently," said Ryan, "but we already knew that."

Miles grimaced. "The beast that comes up out of the abyss will make war."

"Yeah," said Ryan. "The beast."

IT DIDN'T TAKE LONG to get ready because they had nothing besides the clothes they were wearing. Ryan had swapped his torn trainers for a pair of combat boots left behind by one of the deserting soldiers. It made it a little easier to walk without a limp.

The weather was biting, and away from the camp's bonfire, things would certainly become even more uncomfortable. Hopefully, once they got moving – and probably fighting for their lives – their blood would start pumping and things would be bearable. At least they were all wearing jumpers or jackets.

Ryan voiced his concerns one last time. It felt necessary. "Are we sure we want to do this?"

Miles patted him on the back and gave a thin-lipped smile. The female medic had been by earlier with pain relief and fresh bandages, and they were all now a little less worse for wear. "Like I said, lad, I have no choice. You do, though, and I'll understand if you and yer brother back oot of this fight. This isn't yer home."

Ryan shook his head. "We're with you every step of the way."

Cameron grunted. "I'll keep ye safe, English. I'm used to it by now."

"Maybe this time I'll save *you*."

"Stranger things have happened."

Tom moved over to the tent's flap. "If we're going to do this, let's make the most of the sunlight we have left." He looked at his watch. "We have most of the day if we move now."

"Good," said Ryan. "One thing in our favour, at least."

"You think that thing is still out there?" asked Aaron. Everyone knew what he meant. They had all seen the creature outside the petrol station. If not for the army's fortuitous arrival, the beast would have slaughtered Ryan in the middle of the road – and probably everyone else, too. It had been undeniably alien.

And Loobey is a part of it. It absorbed him.

"Of course it's still oot there," said Cameron. "We all saw it run off into the village."

"Best we try to avoid it," said Miles.

Tom huffed. "How exactly do we do that?"

"We keep to the buildings," said Cameron. "Stay low, stay quiet, and hide in the shadows. The enemy is nae that smart, so with a wee bit of common sense, we can get through the village without being seen."

"That's not how things went last time," Tom argued. "We spent most of the time either trapped or running for our lives."

"Aye," Cameron admitted, "but now we know what we're up against. We just need to keep our heids."

Tom exhaled. "Does it concern anybody that Cameron is suddenly the voice of reason?"

Ryan put a hand in the air. "Very much so, but the world's a strange place right now. We'll just have to go with it."

Everyone chuckled.

"Bollocks to ye," said Cameron. "Come on, before I leave yoo eejits behind."

After another brief chuckle, they exited the tent in a line and quickly began to shiver against the cold. Today was chillier than yesterday, and it made Ryan thankful that the army would soon be heading south. While it probably wouldn't be much warmer, it couldn't be as exposed to the elements as the Highlands. To make matters worse, a blustery wind was beginning to gather that promised to make Ryan's ears ache – a sensitivity he inherited from his mam.

Despite its late start, the camp was abuzz with activity. The remaining soldiers hurried back and forth, loading supplies onto trucks and into the back of old, battered jeeps. Half the tents were dismantled, and those that remained had been repitched around a single lit bonfire. Holloway was nowhere to be seen.

Cameron had his pistol out. He held it in both hands and pointed it at the ground like he knew what he was doing. Ryan wondered if they should try to find more weapons, that perhaps some had been left behind by the departing soldiers, but then he realised any soldier going AWOL would most likely want to take their rifle with them.

Cameron scampered in a half crouch towards the road that ran alongside the camp. As usual, the big Scot seemed to be enjoying himself, and his sudden focus was unnerving. Cameron Pollock might not have amounted to much by traditional standards, but Ryan had to admit the man was good to have around in a crisis.

They'd not been given permission to leave the camp, so Ryan half expected to be stopped at any moment. If any of the soldiers noticed them, however, they did nothing about it. They either didn't care, or they didn't want the hassle.

Cameron got everyone onto the road. Being so out in the open made sneaking pointless, so they stood up straight and jogged towards the petrol station up the hill. It was there they finally met resistance. Cameron reached under his jumper to grab the pistol, but Ryan put a hand on his arm and stopped him. "Don't."

Cameron looked to argue, but he changed his mind and nodded. "Aye."

Up close, the army's defensive line was imposing. Sandbags, inert vehicles, and stacks of empty supply crates formed a continuous barrier of several hundred metres, behind which two dozen evenly spaced soldiers watched the village. The two men closest heard Cameron's group and turned around. "The hell yoo feckers doing out here?" one of them bellowed, leaping out of cover and pointing a rifle at them.

"We're heading back into the village," said Cameron, undeterred. He continued approaching, but everyone else slowed to a gradual walk. Tom raised his hands in the air.

"Holloway give ye permission to be oot here?" the soldier demanded.

"Aye," said Cameron. "Gave us a pat on the back, he did. We gunna have a problem here?"

The other soldier broke cover and stood beside his colleague with his own rifle raised. The first soldier moved his eye closer to his scope. "Aye, I reckon we is. Yer telling' me a pack o' lies, pal."

"I ain't your pal, buddy," said Cameron, "and we're getting past whether ye like it or not."

"Not without a bullet in yer heid, yer not."

It dawned on Ryan who they were dealing with. It was Corporal Kay's mate. The private named Dan. Beanie Hat.

Of all the tosspots to run into.

"Please," said Fiona. "There are people still alive in the village. We need to warn them. They need to know this whole place is about to go up in flames."

The soldier raised an eyebrow. "The feck ye talkin' aboot, love?"

"The village. Holloway has orders to raze it to the ground, along with anyone who's still alive."

"There ain't no one left alive in there. We've been calling oot fer days."

Cameron stopped advancing, probably not wanting to push his luck too far. He was twelve feet from Beanie Hat now. "Aye, ye've been calling oot, but nowt's been coming but the greens. Anyone left alive is probably trapped. Yer'd know that if ye actually went looking fer survivors instead of hiding behind yer wee walls."

Beanie Hat's face screwed up furiously. "Unless Holloway clears it, ye ain't getting past, all right? Ye wanna try, be ma guest."

Cameron's hand moved towards the pistol again. This time he was three metres away, and too far for Ryan to stop.

Another soldier approached from further down the defensive line. "Let 'em go, Dan."

Beanie Hat turned his head. "Kay?"

Corporal Kay stepped out onto the road. His eye sockets were a deep purple now, and his nose was wider at the bridge, making him look oddly catlike. A miserable sight, for sure, but his rifle remained pointed at the ground. He seemed in no mood to fight. "Just let 'em go if they want. Who are we to argue?"

"They said the whole place is about to be torched. That true?"

Kay shrugged. "Dunno, but the only thing we *can* do is put a match to this hellhole."

"And we're inclined to agree," said Miles, holding his palms out in peace, "but some of our friends and neighbours are still alive in the village. We need to warn them. How can we not?"

Kay glanced back at the village, sighed, then turned back. "The people in the pub, eh? They would've made it oot on their own by now. Ye want some advice? Go back to yer tents and pray ye live long enough to leave with the rest of us."

"We cannae do that," said Cameron. "It's not in ma blood to back doon."

Kay wrinkled his swollen nose, wincing in pain. "Aye, I know. All right, if ye have to go, then go, but Holloway will probably have us shoot ye on sight once he realises ye've escaped. He's done far worse for far less."

"Thanks fer the warning, pal, but I'll take ma chances."

"I'm not yer pal, buddy, but good luck."

"Aye," said Cameron. "Um, sorry aboot the nose. Ma temper, eh?"

Corporal Kay nodded, turned to the other soldiers to chat for a moment, then walked away. The two remaining soldiers stood aside, rifles lowered. The way ahead was clear. The only thing they had to get past now was Beanie Hat's baleful glare.

Ryan moved beside Cameron, and they approached a narrow gap in the defensive line between a bronze Mini Cooper and a rusty post office van that the soldiers had obviously rolled into place. "We actually got through that with diplomacy," he said as they passed through the barrier. "Cam, I think you're actually growing as a person."

"Don't count on it. I were one second away from whipping oot ma pistol and putting a hole in his face. Come on, English, let's leave these jessies to go back to playing wi' their cocks."

"The feck did ye just say?"

Ryan and the others turned back. Beanie Hat had stepped through the gap after them and was now glaring at them.

Miles, as usual, tried to play peacemaker. "I'm sorry, sir. Is there a problem?"

"Aye, I wanna know what shite just came oot of that ginger rat's mouth."

"We're leaving," said Fiona. "There's no need for trouble."

Cameron started back towards the barrier. His hand moved again towards his hidden pistol. "Ye got a problem, pal?"

Ryan grabbed his arm. "Please, Cameron. Not now."

Cameron scowled at Ryan, and for a moment Ryan worried he was about to get punched. Then the big Scot calmed down. His fists opened up and he let out a sigh. He ceased approaching Beanie Hat and instead gave a lighthearted shrug. "I were just wishin' ye well, pal. Nae harm done, eh?"

Beanie Hat continued to glare, rifle halfway risen. Miles put his hands out to the man in peace. "We're leaving, okay? Thank you for letting us through, my friend."

"I suggest ye get moving while ye still can."

"Yes, yes, of course. Thanks again."

Everyone turned around and started walking.

"Oh," Beanie Hat suddenly barked after them, "and yoo can take this with ye."

Ryan half turned in time to see a flurry of movement as Beanie Hat dropped to one knee, raised his rifle all the way, and squinted down his scope. A sudden *zip* was followed by an ear-rending *crack*.

And then there was complete silence.

Cameron collapsed to the ground.

———

THE GUNSHOT SUMMONED Corporal Kay back to the scene, and he immediately aimed his rifle at Beanie Hat. "Dan! Stand down, ye feckin halfwit!"

Beanie Hat showed no sign of giving a shit about what he'd just done, but he obeyed anyway. He tossed his rifle on the ground and put his hands up lazily. "Needed doin', Corporal. Like Holloway says, it's all big picture stuff now."

Corporal Kay turned and caught Ryan's eye. "Get the fuck oot o' here. Go! Now!"

Ryan looked around and gathered everyone together. "Help me with him," he asked his brother, pointing at Cameron, who was shuddering on the ground. Tom helped the two of them drag him, and they all hurried towards the village.

"The fecker shot me in the arse," Cameron bellowed, breaking clear of his shock. "Right in the feckin' shitter."

"Shut up," said Ryan. "Just... shut up."

They hurried as a group as fast as they could. Cameron weighed as much as a horse, and even with three of them it was an effort to keep moving. Blood stained the big Scot's cargo trousers all the way down the back of his left thigh. He had indeed been shot in the arse. Was Dan a poor shot, or had this been his intention? It was a humiliation and Cameron was alive to suffer it.

"Ma feckin' arse."

"It's going to be okay, Cameron," said Fiona. "We've got you."

"Ma feckin' arse."

"All right, Cameron," said Miles, shushing him. "Let us get ye somewhere safe."

"We're going in the wrong direction for that," said Tom unhelpfully.

"Over here," said Chloe, pointing ahead and veering across the road. "Ma house is right over there."

Ryan looked around, waiting for the greens to suddenly emerge from the side streets and crevices, but right now the village seemed deserted. Nothing was alive within a hundred metres of the soldier's defensive line.

That didn't mean everything was safe, though.

Green fungus sprouted everywhere, poking between paving slabs and filling the cracks in the road. The more Ryan looked, the more he realised it was growing everywhere that rainwater collected.

The windows of the nearest houses were shattered, no doubt struck by the soldier's rifle fire during the last few days. The petrol station behind them was completely ransacked, its inventory picked clean by the army. Several dead greens lay scattered on the road, riddled with bullet holes. An acidic stench filled the air.

Chloe turned her nose up and groaned. "They're dissolving. Look!"

While continuing to struggle with a pain-wracked Cameron, Ryan studied the nearest body lying on the road. It was impossible to tell whether it had been male or female, young or old, but it had at least been human. The torso was flat, blanketed in dark green fuzz turning black in places. A pair of limp tendrils spread out on the asphalt, sharp talons marking their ends. A viscous green puddle spread beneath the body, bubbling slightly as if a chemical reaction were taking place. It really did seem like the corpse was dissolving.

"It stinks," said Cameron, showing his teeth. "Bloody rotten."

"Can we hurry?" said Tom, starting to turn red in the face as he battled to keep hold of Cameron. "I don't want to catch a bullet in *my* backside."

"None of us do," said Aaron. "Just keep moving."

"I'm gunna kill the bastard," Cameron shouted. "He shot me in the arse."

Ryan grunted. "Yeah, you've mentioned it once or twice."

"He'll pay for his sins," said Miles. "Such unnecessary violence."

"I'll show the bastard unnecessary violence," said Cameron.

"And I'll be right by your side," said Ryan, realising that he was furious.

I'm furious that someone shot my mate. Cameron is my mate.

What the hell?

"Cheers, English. Ye can hold ma beer while I throttle the wee bastard."

"Everything is breaking down," said Fiona. "The army isn't going to help anyone. They don't care."

"Over here," said Chloe. "Hurry." Everyone followed her to a short terrace of three narrow houses, each with tiny front gardens. The windows on these properties were still intact – out of the soldier's firing line.

"This is your place?" asked Aaron. He was clearly terror-stricken, but unlike his previous visit to the village, he remained in control of himself. He had found a way to master his fear. Ryan felt a twinge of pride as he realised his little brother had become a man.

"Aye, this ma home," said Chloe, and she rushed up to the front door with her keys jangling. She unlocked it and shouldered it open, hurrying inside. No one waited to receive an invitation, and they all rushed in after her.

"Mam?" Chloe shouted in a tiny living room with exposed floorboards. "Mam, are you here?"

Miles slammed the door behind, and Ryan, Tom, and Aaron bundled Cameron onto a nearby sofa. It was upholstered in navy blue polyester, but it would soon be stained with blood.

"Mam, are you in here?" Chloe shouted again. "Mam?"

It quickly became clear that the house was empty. The realisation sent Chloe into a glum silence.

"That fascist bastard shot me in the feckin'—"

"Arse," said Ryan. "Yeah, we got it, mate. Let us take a look."

Cameron stopped his moaning for a second and looked at Ryan with wide-open eyes. "Ye finally gettin' what ye want, eh, English? A good wee gander at ma backside."

"You've got me," said Ryan. "It's all I've been able to think about. Ye wee bawbag!"

Cameron burst into laughter, but it soon turned back to moans. He was sweating profusely. His lip was bleeding where he had bit down. Ryan guiltily recalled his conversation about Cameron rushing head first into danger and never getting injured. The one time he had chosen to walk away from a fight, he'd been shot.

"He had no reason to do this," said Ryan, still fuming. "You walked away."

"Aye," said Miles. "I'm proud of ye, Cameron Pollock. Ye did the right thing."

Cameron opened his mouth, yet seemed unable to speak. He was weak, almost childlike for a moment, but then he scowled. "And look where it feckin' got me. Shot in the feckin' arse." He pulled the pistol out of his waistband and handed it to Ryan. It was heavier than he would have expected. "Ye shoulda let me use that."

"It would only have made things worse."

"Maybe."

"I'll fetch some towels," said Chloe. "I think I have painkillers somewhere too."

"I'll come help you," said Fiona, turning her head. "Too much blood in here."

"A needle and thread too," said Miles. "This is nae gunna be pretty."

"Talk aboot ye own arse," said Cameron. "Ye can do a lot worse than mine."

"It's not a contest," said Ryan.

"But if it were, ye'd lose every time, English."

Ryan chuckled.

Chloe returned a minute later with a bundle of towels with a packet of painkillers perched on top. There was also a bottle of what looked like tequila. She set everything down on a cheap wooden coffee table and started handing it out. Ryan took the towels and wedged them underneath Cameron's hip, not that there was any chance to save the sofa. "I need you to unbutton your trousers and pull them down."

Cameron grumbled obscenities, but he did what he was told, and cheered when Chloe handed him the bottle of tequila. "Eighteenth birthday present," she explained.

"Many happy returns," said Cameron, and then downed a quarter of the bottle in one go.

Fiona came back into the room with a small tin the size of a paperback novel and asked Chloe about it. "This it?"

"Yeah, that's the one. There should be a needle and thread in there."

"Give it here," said Miles, reaching out a hand. "And save some of that alcohol, Cameron. Do you hear me?"

Ryan tugged Cameron's trousers down to expose his wounded buttock. There was so much blood that it looked like he sweated it from every pore. A dark gash tore through the centre of his cheek, small enough that it appeared only as a minor injury.

"We need to get the bullet out, right?" asked Ryan. "Or it'll get infected."

"Not necessarily," said Miles. "Yer've been watching too many films. The lack of boiling water and antiseptic is what will likely cause infection. The bullet can stay in there for now."

Cameron grunted in pain.

Miles shushed him, then rooted around the tin Fiona had given him. He pulled out a spool of black thread and a darning needle.

"You know how to do this?" asked Tom. He had taken a seat in an old rocking chair in the corner of the room. He played the part of the old woman well.

"Aye, I've closed a wound or two in ma time."

"When?" asked Aaron, standing with his back against the front door. "You're a vicar, not a doctor."

Miles glanced at the floor, then at the needle and thread in his hands. "I spent nine months in Sierra Leone working for the Christian Mission." He laughed gently. "I were a younger man in them days. Braver. Foolish. Fifty thousand died in that country's civil war, so believe me when I say I saw ma fair share of gunshot wounds. At first, I would just assist the doctors and nurses whenever a patient came in, but by the time I left I was sewing up wounds and setting broken bones all by ma self. So many dying young men came through it was more like a production line than a hospital. Most didn't make it." He let out a long sigh. "That was the first and only time I ever served the Lord overseas. Figured I'd done my bit and it were okay to enjoy the pleasures of home."

Ryan smiled sadly. "I'm glad you're here with us now, Miles."

"Aye, me too, lad. Feels like I was meant to be here at this moment, with all of yoo."

"Can yoo feckers hurry up and see to ma arse?" said Cameron. He took another swig of tequila and almost choked. "Make it quick."

Aaron moved away from the front door, skin ashen. He was shaking his head and staring at the needle and thread between Miles's fingers. "I'm not sure I can stomach this. Is it okay if I leave the room?"

Ryan nodded. "Of course, little brother. I might have to join you if it gets too grizzy."

"Jessies," said Cameron, rolling his eyes.

Standing nearby, Chloe put a hand on Aaron's wrist and pointed out of the living room door. Upon entering, Ryan had briefly glanced a dining area with a staircase leading upstairs, and a kitchen and bathroom at the rear of the house. It was an odd layout. Narrow. "Ye can go lie down in ma room if ye want," she said. "It's the door on the right at the top of the stairs."

Aaron nodded at her. "Cheers. I just feel a bit sick, you know?"

Ryan watched his brother leave, then returned his focus to Miles. "How can I help?"

"Keep Cameron relaxed."

"How the hell do I do that?"

"Sing to me," said Cameron. "Let's hear a wee bit of them Spice Gals yoo English are so proud of."

Ryan chuckled. "Things would have to be a lot worse than they are right now, mate."

Miles threaded the needle and raised it. "Cameron, hand that booze to Ryan. We need to sterilise the wound as best we can."

Cameron passed the bottle over, but added a warning too. "Dinnae waste it, pal."

Ryan trickled the tequila on the large gash on Cameron's buttock. It washed away enough blood to reveal a gleaming white butt cheek. "Bloody hell, Cam, you need to get yourself a tan."

"Up here," said Miles, "this *is* a tan. Okay, Cameron, hold yer breath. That's it, and… *release.*"

Cameron gritted his teeth and hissed as Miles pierced his flesh with the needle. Ryan had to look away – it was a little too intense – but he also wanted to help Cameron through this, so he did the unexpected. Clearing his throat, he began, "*If you wanna be my lover…*"

Cameron bellowed with laughter. "Aye, that's it, English! Hey, Posh Spice, join in."

Tom rolled his eyes. "I'll pass, thank you very much."

"Keep it down," Fiona hissed. She was standing near the living room's single window and peering out through the net curtain. "We don't know how close the greens are. Let's not announce our presence, huh?"

Ryan stopped singing. Cameron stopped laughing. They looked at each other like two schoolboys caught talking in class.

Miles concentrated.

Aaron re-entered the room suddenly, looking queasier than ever. Ryan's stomach twanged with fear.

He's infected.

They don't always know.

Ryan jumped up and moved over to the door. "Aaron, what is it?"

"Nothing. Can I just talk to you for a minute?" His voice was flat, emotionless. Or perhaps he was merely trying to keep himself calm. Either way, Ryan had known his little brother long enough to know that something was up.

"All right, man, I'm coming." He walked out of the room with Aaron, and was about to ask him what was wrong, when Aaron put a finger to his lips and pointed to the stairs.

Ryan's bad feeling only grew worse as he silently followed his brother up the stairs to a tiny landing. His combat boots clonked loudly and made him wince. On the landing, Aaron entered a door on the right. The smell of death was something Ryan was used to, but he hadn't been expecting it now. The bedroom clearly belonged to Chloe. The walls were decorated in garish pinks and deep purples. A woman with stringy blonde hair lay on a double bed in the middle of the room, head propped against a faux-leather headboard. If not for the grey, sagging flesh around the woman's murky eyeballs, one might have mistaken her for sleeping.

Aaron picked something up from the bedside table. A foil packet. He studied it intently. "Looks like she overdosed. *Zopiclone.* What's that?"

"No idea. You should put it down though. Don't touch anything."

Aaron shrugged. "Why not?"

"I don't know. It just feels like we shouldn't touch anything. This is obviously Chloe's mam."

Aaron nodded. "She must have thought Chloe was dead and came into her room to be closer to her."

Ryan covered his face with a hand, terrified by the thought of his own mother doing the same. "This is fucking horrible. Chloe doesn't even know."

"We need to tell her."

Ryan nodded.

"Ryan?"

"Yeah?"

"Do you think mam is okay? Holloway said the fungus has spread everywhere. I don't think Manchester is safe any more."

"I don't either. It probably never was. The only thing I do know is that our family is tough." He held up his bandaged forearm, reminding himself of how much damage he had taken without dying. "Mam's a survivor, just like you and me. Sophie too. Tomorrow morning, we're out of here, and we ain't gunna stop until we get home. Mam and Sophie are alive, Aaron, I know it. I promise, you'll see them again. I promise, you'll make it home." He reached into his pocket. "I wrote them both a letter, but I'm going to read it to them in person."

Aaron looked down at Chloe's mother and sighed. "But what if they think we're dead? What if they assume we're never coming home?"

Ryan put a hand on his brother's shoulder and pulled him into a hug. "Then we're going to give them the biggest surprise of their lives. Come on, we need to think about Chloe right now. She's going to need us."

The two brothers left the dead woman in peace.

6

"We can't leave," said Ed. "Those things will kill us."

"Or infect us," said somebody else.

"My Brian is out there. What's happened to him?"

"I need to get home."

Oliver shook his head, sitting at the bar. "I don't wanna become one of those monsters."

Dale pounded the butt of his shotgun against a table to shut everyone up. His eyes were like vats of acid, ready to burn anyone who caught his gaze. "We stay here, we die. I dinnae know aboot the rest o' ye, but I'd rather fight than lie down like a wee slag. Those things outside ma pub are flesh, bone, and blood, nae different to the rest of us. Have some backbone, will ye nae?"

Helen sighed. She didn't like the way she was sat at the table closest to Dale, as if she were his lady in his mad little fiefdom. Less than a week and he already thought of these people as *his*. The horror had turned everybody meek. "Dale's right," she said reluctantly, hating to admit it. She had considered what he'd said about help not coming and could see no way to disagree. The army was nearby, but they had done nothing to enter the village. They weren't here to save anybody.

Shelly gasped. "Helen, yoo know how bad it is oot there more than any of us. It would be insane to leave."

Helen took in a long breath, anger, rage, sadness and spite bubbling away beneath her skin. Her soul was empty. "Aye, I know better than anyone what's oot there. I watched ma wee daffodil get butchered. His blood is still beneath ma fingernails."

"So why the hell do ye want to go outside?" asked Oliver, his incredulous face begging to be punched. "We're safe here."

"We all thought we were safe at the kirk, too," she said, "and the bowls club. Yer all fools if ye think ye can just stay here and wait for everything to blow over. Those things will get inside. Then they'll slice yer throats open and leave ye to bleed out on these ugly carpets. Honestly, I don't give two fecks what any of ye do, but I'll nae sit here and wait to die. I'm going outside to kill as many of those bastards as I can."

Dale grinned. "Now there's a battle cry. Ye heard the lass, there's nae option to stay safe and cosy. We die here or we fight to live."

"I'll die here, thanks very much," said Oliver. "I've still got some sense left."

Dale's grin remained, but it cracked slightly, became a distortion. He marched over to Oliver and stood over him. Oliver leant back on his stool, eyelids flickering like he expected to get punched. "Ye've got a problem there, pal, because this is ma pub and I'm calling last orders. Get ready to leave."

"No," said Oliver. "I'll nae throw ma life away so yoo can play general. It's a death sentence. We should all stay here until there's nae another option."

"Yeah," said Ed. "We don't have to leave right now, do we?"

There was a mumble of assent. Ed and Oliver weren't the only ones who wanted to stay. They were all cowards, afraid to take responsibility for their own lives. Helen hated them. Before this week, she'd never hated anyone.

Dale glared at Ed. "Have ye seen that monster outside? It's bigger than a highland cow, and getting bigger all the time. There are more greens gathering every minute. If we dinnae leave now, we're fecked. Don't ye fools get it, ye feckin' wee gobshites?"

"We should vote," said Oliver, rising slightly on his stool. "Nobody put you in charge, Dale. We don't have to listen to you."

Dale's grin distorted further, now the smirk of a hungry cat eyeing a mouse. "That right, now, is it?"

"Yes! We all have a right to—"

Dale struck like a viper, body moving all at once and without warning. He brought up his shotgun and smashed the butt into the centre of Oliver's face, knocking the startled man backwards off his stool and onto the floor. There was a nasty clonk as his head struck the cement beneath the threadbare carpet. Surprisingly, he wasn't knocked out. He rolled onto his side and tried to get up.

Everyone was screaming. Ed was begging. Helen was numb. She'd been waiting for this.

Dale lifted the shotgun and brought the stock down on the back of Oliver's head as the man tried to crawl away. The blow succeeded in knocking him unconscious, but Dale wasn't done. He brought the shotgun down on Oliver's head another three times until his skull shattered and his brains leaked out of his ears.

Everyone cried out in horror.

Shelly threw up. Ed wept like a child.

Helen stared, unflinchingly, at the monster who had given her Andy.

Any goodness inside him went into my boy. These people need to get as far away from Dale as they can.

Dale was panting and grinning like a madman. Oliver's blood stained his face. He looked around the room, at each person in turn. "I'm afraid Oliver's been barred. Anyone want to join him?"

Nobody did.

CAMERON WAS SO DRUNK, he struggled to keep his eyes open. Now and then, he would catch himself falling asleep and jolt awake, but gradually he was losing the battle. Miles had stitched up his buttock and dressed it with packing tape and a cut-up tea towel. With so much booze in his system, it was decided that Cameron could cope without painkillers. The bullet remained firmly lodged in his cheek, but Miles once again confirmed it was not a pressing concern.

Chloe was a mess, sobbing in the kitchen. Miles and Fiona tried to soothe her. Aaron watched her from the living room doorway, his expression full of pity. He clearly had a crush on the girl, but he was setting himself up for disappointment. Even if Aaron hadn't been fifteen, he still wouldn't be Chloe's type. Maybe he was hoping she would make an exception.

We need to get you laid, brother.

Ryan sat in the lounge on the floor by the window, holding Cameron's pistol. A radiator hung beneath the window, but it didn't work. Somehow, the taps were still giving cold water, so everyone sipped from mismatched glasses, taking advantage of running H_2O while they still had the chance.

"We can't stay here much longer," said Tom. He hadn't moved from the rocking chair since arriving an hour ago. He'd grown pale, and his knees bobbed up and down like pistons. "We don't want to get stuck here in the dark. We certainly don't want to be here when the army starts torching the place."

"I know," said Ryan, "but what can we do? Cameron's paralytic, and Chloe needs some time to process that her mam is... gone."

"We don't have the luxury of compassion right now. The clock is ticking."

Ryan exhaled through his nostrils and nodded. "Another half hour and we'll get moving. There'll be plenty of light left."

"Okay. Hopefully we can sober Cameron up enough to walk. I hate to admit it, but the man's too useful to leave behind."

"I know what you mean. People can surprise you, huh? Even

Miles isn't exactly what I would have expected. Definitely not how I pictured your everyday vicar."

Tom chuckled. "I heard him call Cameron a *fannybaws* earlier. I'm not even sure what that means." They both laughed, but Tom grew serious. "You're surprising, too, Ryan. Even after all these years."

"Really? How?"

Tom shrugged. "For years I saw you as, I don't know... *lost*, I suppose – and afraid. Afraid of facing life. Afraid of tying yourself to any one career. Of starting a family. All of it. And before you take offence, I don't mean it as badly as it sounds. I'm just saying that I've always thought of you as a free spirit, someone who would never succumb to responsibility or routine."

Ryan *was* offended despite the warning, but he also agreed in a way. "You're right. I always felt like I wouldn't amount to anything, so I suppose I tried to delay having to grow up for as long as possible. Now, I'll never get the chance to be mundane."

"No, I suppose you won't, but honestly, this madness suits you well. You might never have achieved anything before, but that's all changed. Now you're rushing into danger to help strangers, fighting monsters and making plans. You've been injured in every part of your body, but you keep on going. Heroes really are forged in battle."

Ryan chuckled. "You calling me a hero?"

"That's exactly what I'm saying. I might not agree with most of your reckless decisions, but I can't deny your courage. You keep thanking these people for saving your life – but don't you realise that you've saved theirs too? You never give up on anyone, Ryan, and I admire that. Perhaps I even envy it."

Ryan reached out a hand and waited for Tom to take it. He did and the two men shook. "You're one of my oldest friends, Tom, and I love you."

Tom nodded. "The feeling's mutual. I'm sorry for the last few days. They haven't been my best."

"I'm sorry, too. Let's just make the days ahead count for something, yeah?"

Tom nodded. "From now on, I've got your back, I promise."

"I know that, man."

Cameron had fallen asleep, and he announced it with a wet fart that made both of them wince.

"That's rank," said Aaron, still standing in the doorway. He covered his face in the crook of his elbow.

Ryan did the same. "Are you surprised? We've all seen how the guy eats." He pointed the pistol at the sleeping Scot. "I should shoot him."

Rifle fire cracked outside and startled them.

Ryan flinched. He then rolled onto his knees and crawled over to the window. He peered beneath the net curtain and tried to get a look outside. Tom slid out of the rocking chair and crouched beside him. "Do you see anything?"

"No, it must be the soldiers at the barrier. The greens must be close by. We need to—"

Something struck the window hard enough to crack it.

Ryan leapt back and fell onto his butt. "W-What the hell?"

Something struck the window again, adding tributaries to the crack. Although rendered blurry by the net curtain, Ryan saw clearly what was on the other side of the glass.

A green pressed its face against the window, talons whipping back and forth either side of it.

"The window's going to shatter," said Tom. "It's only single-glazed."

Everyone appeared in the living room and started to panic as the window finally shattered. The net curtains lifted as a blustery wind came inside.

Ryan shoved the pistol under his belt and grabbed Cameron's arm. He tried to rouse him. "Wake up! Cameron, on your feet."

Cameron mumbled, his eyes half-open. Aaron and Tom helped Ryan lift the man, and they pulled him to his feet. He was a drunken mess, and he didn't even come to when they moved him quickly into the dining room.

"The back door," said Chloe. Her eyes were red with spent tears. "It leads to an alleyway. The pub is right at the end of it."

"What if there's more of them out there?" asked Tom.

"Then we'll deal with them," said Ryan. "It's what we were expecting. We can do this."

Everyone hurried through the narrow house, going from the dining room into the galley-style kitchen, before funnelling towards a back door in a small space outside the bathroom. The key was hanging in the lock, so Chloe turned it and yanked it open. She stepped backwards onto Aaron's foot, but there was no time for him to get upset about it. They all spilled out onto a postage stamp of a patio, where there was nothing except a table and two cast-iron chairs. Ryan wished there had been a petrol mower or a chainsaw to go at the greens with, horror-movie style, but he knew that was too much to ask.

I'm really not the man I used to be.

Chloe opened the back gate into the alleyway, and when Ryan stepped out into it, he was surprised to find it familiar. It was the same alleyway the beast had chased Aaron through, and the body of the dead woman Ryan had found was still lying there, rotting on the pavement.

Chloe saw the corpse and yelped. "Carol. Oh no, Carol."

Aaron touched her arm. "Was she a friend of yours?"

"Just a neighbour. She taught piano."

"There's no time to mourn," said Miles. He pointed to the end of the alleyway, to where a pair of greens had appeared. They were already making their way closer, bouncing to and fro between the two sets of garden walls.

Everyone headed towards the other end of the alleyway, towards the pub. The wheelie bins were all knocked over, and Ryan knew they'd been tipped by the beast when it had pursued his brother.

But where was the beast now?

They struggled to keep Cameron moving. He was still out of it, chatting nonsense, and did little to help himself. "Come on, Cameron," Ryan pleaded. "Wake the hell up."

"How did they know we were inside," said Fiona. "Did they see us through the window?"

"No way," said Ryan. "I was sitting on the floor. Tom was in the rocking chair. When I looked out the window, it was already right there."

"They set us up," said Aaron. "What's the one advantage we have over them?" No one replied, so he gave them the answer. "We're faster than they are. When they attack us, we have the option to run away. Instead of attacking us as soon as we entered the village, they let us pile up inside Chloe's house where they could pen us in."

"And now we're stuck in an alley," said Miles, his expression turning dour.

More greens spilled into the alleyway behind them, but several had also appeared ahead. Aaron was right. They *had* been set up, and both ends of the alleyway were now blocked.

Fiona skidded to a halt. "What do we do?"

"We have to fight," said Ryan. "There's no other choice."

"Fight with what?" asked Tom, struggling to hold Cameron upright. "We have nothing."

"Bleach," said Aaron. "Gerard said we can hurt the greens with bleach."

"Great! I'll just get that bottle out of my pocket."

"There's bleach in the bathroom cupboard," said Chloe.

Miles loosed a litany of curses that would have made any of the soldiers back at camp blush. "Everyone, back into the garden."

Everyone changed direction, funnelling their way back into Chloe's tiny garden. They had left the back door to the house hanging wide open. Tom let go of Cameron and hurried forward.

Ryan yelled out as he and his brother were forced to carry more weight. "Whoa, Tom, what are you doing?"

"Thought I'd try being a hero for once." He rushed back into the house.

"He doesn't even know where to look," said Miles.

"There's only one cupboard in the bathroom," said Chloe. "He can't miss it."

Fiona started pacing the small garden. "What if the greens have made it inside?"

"I'm going in to help him," said Chloe, and before anybody could argue, she sprinted back inside her house after Tom.

All was quiet.

The back gate started to rattle. Miles swore and threw himself against it. A sturdy stone wall made up most the garden's perimeter, so if the greens were going to get in, it would be through the gate.

Ryan couldn't hold Cameron's weight any more, so he set the drunken fool down on one of the cast-iron chairs and then arched his back with relief. He had forgotten about the bullet wound in the man's backside, and Cameron yelped in pain. "Argh, ye dopey bastard."

"Cameron, you need to wake up, man."

Cameron rubbed at his eyes and looked around blearily. "Are we as screwed as it looks?"

Ryan glanced at Miles, battling against the rattling fence. "Yeah, I think we're in a bad spot, mate."

Chloe's screams echoed from inside the house.

"And getting worse." Ryan moved towards the door, but his brother cut in front of him.

"Hold on," Aaron shouted, sprinting for the back door, but before he had a chance to go inside, Chloe hurtled backwards over the step and collided with him. The two of them went sprawling onto the patio.

A green moved into the doorway. It tried to whip its talons, but the doorway was too narrow and it failed, clumsily hitting the wooden frame.

Ryan rushed to help his brother. He pulled out the pistol and pulled the trigger, but it didn't budge and nothing happened. "What the—?"

Miles called out from the garden gate.

The green stumbled out of the doorway, its talons now finding room to swing. Aaron and Ryan instinctively grabbed Chloe and rolled the girl out of harm's way, but it was too late to escape the danger themselves.

The green curled back its talons. Its face was half-burnt, a possible victim of Ryan's church arson.

Then the monster squealed.

A heady stench filled the air like a hospital ward. Flesh and chemicals.

The green thrashed like a wounded rat, its talon whipping at the air wildly. Aaron and Ryan clambered across the patio to avoid getting sliced.

Tom appeared in the doorway behind the green, which was now producing smoky tendrils like it was about to go up in flames. In Tom's hand, he held a large yellow bottle made from plastic. A flick of his wrist sent a fresh stream of liquid onto the green's back, summoning fresh squeals. Until now, Ryan had not heard the greens make any sounds at all.

Tom kicked the green in the spine and sent it flopping onto the patio. There, it went still, its flesh sizzling and giving off more smoky black tendrils. Dozens of bugs tumbled from its body, curled up and died.

Tom went back inside the house, returning a moment later with a second bottle of bleach. He handed it to Ryan just as Ryan got to his feet. "Looks like we found a way to fight back," he said.

Ryan unscrewed the childproof cap with a grim smile. The noxious fumes made his nose tickle, but it was a good smell. It was the smell of something that was going to help them survive. He noticed Tom was trembling. "How's it feel to be a hero, mate?"

"Not bad. Not that good either."

Miles called out again. The gate was beginning to crack and splinter. One of the wooden boards had snapped at the top, revealing thrashing talons beyond. "I cannae keep ma back to this thing much longer, folks."

"Open it," said Ryan, holding the bleach up. "It's time to fight back."

Miles was wheezing, and for a moment he seemed to freeze. Then he leapt away from the garden gate and rushed towards the house. Chloe locked the back door and left the keys dangling. "We dinnae need the feckers coming at us from behind."

"Good thinking," said Ryan. He limped alongside Tom to the front of the group, both of them holding their bleach bottles out in front of them. They focused on the rattling gate.

It only took a few moments for it to burst open.

The greens piled into the tiny garden, which made it easy for Tom and Ryan to soak them with their streams of bleach. The effect was immediate. The greens squealed and thrashed, losing all motivation to attack. The thick emerald fuzz covering their bodies instantly blackened and curled in on itself as some kind of rapid chemical reaction was taking place. A few seconds of suffering was all it took before the greens flopped lifelessly to the ground.

"We have it," said Fiona in awe as she stared at three sizzling corpses. "We finally have a way to fight back. We can beat these fucking things."

"I'll drink to that," said Cameron, listing precariously in his chair.

More greens appeared in the gateway. A lot of them.

"I would nae count our chickens yet," said Miles.

Ryan and Tom glanced at each other. Tom nodded. "Let's get to work."

———

TOM AND RYAN stumbled into the alleyway, panting and grunting. A pile of greens lay on the patio behind them. The bleach had burned through their flesh like acetylene torches. The only problem was that Ryan's bottle was already more than half empty, and Tom had been even more liberal with his.

Everyone huddled behind Ryan and Tom. Cameron was now moving of his own accord, but he was still severely drunk with a bullet lodged in his arse. Every step forward involved half a step sideways. Fiona and Miles did their best to keep him moving in the right direction, but it was a constant battle.

Greens spilled into the alleyway from both ends, slow and clumsy but determined. If Ryan and the others moved quickly enough, they might be able to make it out before their exit was completely blocked.

"Come on," said Ryan. "We need to get out of this goddamn alleyway."

They hurried as fast as they could, Ryan and Tom dousing the nearest greens with bleach. Their agonised thrashing caused them to knock against each other and fall down. It created an opening. Letting loose another stream of bleach, Ryan moved through the widening gap at the end of the alleyway. The others kept pace with him and they made it into the open area between the village's post office and pub. Once again, Ryan spotted his lifeless Audi sitting in the car park, only this time its rear windscreen was coated in green fuzz. The stuff seemed to be growing everywhere, even out of the drain covers at the sides of the road.

Greens surrounded the old pub. A hundred or more. They huddled together, bumping each other and scuffing their feet on the ground as they walked. Several were blackened and burnt, more casualties of the fire Ryan had set at the church.

An almighty roar assaulted the air.

Ryan saw the fear in Aaron's eyes, and followed his brother's gaze until he saw what he was looking at. The beast.

The massive, fuzz-covered abomination had grown twice as large since the last time they'd encountered it, and it no longer walked on two legs. Instead, it lumbered on four fat appendages. It resembled a giant version of the bugs. More disembodied heads hung from its bulbous torso, and Ryan's legs almost deserted him when he saw Loobey's face still among them.

"They're everywhere," Cameron slurred. "Feckin' gobshites."

Ryan grabbed his drunken companion but had nowhere to direct him. The alleyway behind them was filling up fast from the other end. He looked at the pistol in his hand and thought about using it. Instead, he handed it back to Cameron. "You're bloody gun is broken. I tried to use it but the trigger is stuck."

Cameron examined it briefly then raised an eyebrow. "Did you take off the safety?"

"The what now?"

With a half-drunk grin, Cameron thumbed at the pistol, aimed it down the alleyway, and fired. The blast echoed, and fifteen metres away, a green stumbled backwards. "Seems to be working fine to me, English."

"We have to get to the pub," said Fiona. Her hair had come loose from her ponytail on one side. It gave her a slightly mad quality.

Ryan looked towards the pub and saw an upper window hanging open. A shadow loomed there, watching them. Someone was inside. "Get as close as you can," he shouted. "Get to the pub. Tom, we need to make a path."

Tom's flesh seemed to hang off his skull. Ryan had never seen him so utterly mortified. Despite his fear, he nodded and got moving. The two of them flicked their bottles of bleach, burning the greens in front of them. As before, it completely distracted the monsters from attacking, and killed several within seconds. The chemical seemed to cause them to suffer some kind of massive shock. Whatever organism had taken over the people of Choirikell, it could not tolerate bog cleaner at all.

The old pub lay twenty metres ahead, its stone walls and hardwood window frames promising protection within. A dozen greens blocked Ryan's path, but together they might be able to make it.

But what if the people inside the pub refuse to let us in like last time? What if they throw more glasses at us?

They won't. It would alert the greens to their presence.

So would helping us.

Ryan was prepared to smash his way inside the pub if it came to it. He came here to warn the people inside, risking his life to save a group of strangers.

Maybe Tom's right. I am *a hero.*

Nope, probably just an idiot.

More greens succumbed to the bleach-based onslaught, and the pub became more and more within reach. Its windows were all covered by thick drapes, which made it even more likely that people were inside.

Then Tom panicked. He turned his bleach bottle upside down and nothing came out. "It's all gone. What do we do?"

As if sensing an advantage, a nearby green shambled towards Tom. Ryan flicked his wrist overhead like he was wielding a sword and unleashed a thick stream of bleach. The green wheeled back, squealing in agony. Tom stumbled backwards, startled but safe.

More greens came, closing in on all sides. Only Ryan had a means to defend himself, and it was going to run out very soon. A quarter-bottle left. He tried to flick the bleach sparingly, knowing that a small amount was enough to do the job, but after a few seconds it was gone. Half a dozen greens still remained between him and the pub. They weren't going to make it.

We should have stayed at the camp.

I should have had a stag do in Manchester.

Everyone bunched together, back to back. At least they were together.

"We're screwed," said Tom.

"Stay together," Chloe shouted.

"Don't give up," said Fiona. "Fight!"

Cameron took a drunken swing and struck a green in the face. It knocked the creature backwards, but was nowhere near as effective as bleach. The green recovered quickly and whipped its talons at Cameron. Somehow, Cameron's drunkenness helped him. He lost his footing and staggered sideways into Chloe, narrowly avoiding being whipped. "Ma arse is killing me," he complained.

The green whipped at Cameron again, but this time he ducked, collapsing drunkenly onto his knees. The talon sliced the air right above his head and carried on, catching Chloe right across the side of her face. She shrieked in pain and grabbed at her temple.

Cameron saw what had happened and bellowed like a madman. He leapt up and grabbed the green by the skull, screamed into its face and pressing his thumbs into its eye sockets. Then he wrenched the thing's neck so hard that it cracked like a gunshot.

Aaron cried out. "Chloe!"

Miles grabbed Cameron and yanked him back just as a second green appeared and sliced at his neck. The talon whistled in the air, only inches away from his Adam's apple.

"God help us all."

"Fuck God," Cameron roared.

The beast appeared amongst the greens. Its multiple, hanging skulls screamed in silent agony as it lumbered forward, picking up speed. It charged right through the green mob, knocking bodies aside like skittles. It was faster than before – a bloodthirsty rhino – and there would be no outrunning it this time.

Ryan grabbed Aaron and yanked his brother behind him. Tom dropped his empty bleach bottle to the ground and seemed to accept his fate. Chloe sobbed into Fiona's arms, both women closing their eyes and refusing to watch their own deaths. Miles and Cameron raised their fists, ready to go down fighting.

Ryan did nothing.

It's over.

My life never even got started.

The beast bounded towards them.

An almighty blast rang out.

Ryan's ears filled with painful ringing.

The beast collapsed onto its chest. Its momentum caused it to skid along the ground for another ten feet. One of the disembodied heads hanging from its torso popped like a cantaloupe and leaked soapy pink fluids in a trail behind it.

The greens were all seizing, their bodies locked into spasms.

The loud noise.

Ryan had no idea what was happening, but a second almighty blast renewed the ringing in his ears and caused him to duck. A massive chunk of the beast's fuzz-coloured flesh split open, green and black fluids slopping onto the ground. The beast groaned, clearly stunned, but already it was starting to rise.

Somebody grabbed Ryan's arm. He panicked, fearing something had whipped him, but what he saw shocked him. He tried to speak but could barely hear his own voice. "H-Helen?"

Helen glared at Ryan with as much hatred as ever. She held a dark-bladed machete in her right hand, and for a moment he was sure she was about to bury it in his chest. Instead, a flicker of conflict flashed though her eyes, and she dragged Ryan towards the pub.

A small group of armed survivors arrived from around the back of the pub. They looked terrified and weak – all except one. A tall, bony-faced man stood at the front of the group with a smoking shotgun nestled against his shoulder. There was a feral look about him, cheeks craggy and pockmarked. A gold hoop hung from one ear. The look he gave Ryan was unsettling, and the way he expertly loaded shotgun shells into the open barrel of his weapon made it clear he was no stranger to firearms. He nodded to Ryan as Helen dragged him over. "Yoo must be Ryan, eh? I've heard a lot about ye. I'm Dale Finley."

7

D ale fired his shotgun at a nearby green, obliterating its torso. Despite coming to the rescue, the man did not seem friendly. Something about him reeked of *violence*, like a smiling inmate on death row. His expression didn't soften at all, until he eyed Cameron. "Pollock? Is that yoo, ye big bag of shite?"

Cameron beamed, still drunk, but sobering up all the time. He embraced the other man in a hug. "Dale Finley? The king is alive."

"Aye, nowt can kill me, pal. We were aboot to get oota here for good. Luckily, we were still around to pull yer backsides away from the flame."

Miles rolled his eyes. "It's good to see more folk alive, even the likes of yoo, Dale Finley."

"Aye. Sorry about last time, Vicar. The glass-throwing incident." He motioned to Miles's eye patch. "Helen's broken up about it."

He turned to Helen. "It's already forgotten, lass."

Helen's hard exterior wavered for a second. "Thank you."

"Chloe's hurt," said Fiona. "We need to help her."

Dale glanced at her. "She got sliced. Lass is done for."

Chloe sobbed. All the while, the greens continued closing in around them. The beast was getting back to its feet, injured but not beaten. They needed to get out of there now.

"We need to go inside," said Fiona. "I was infected too, but we found a way. We need to help her."

"Leave her," said Dale. "We're getting out of here."

Ryan glanced at Helen. She was looking at Chloe with concern. There was mercy in her. "We can try to save her, Helen," he said. "You know it. You've seen it."

Dale growled. "No feckin' way. Ma pub is closed. We're leaving."

"No," said Helen. "We're going to help Chloe. Then we can leave."

The expression on Dale's face was volcanic. His cheeks quivered, and he glared at Helen as if trying to psychically compel her to obey. When Helen failed to shy away from his stare, he swore. "Fine, but if we lose our chance to leave, I'll kill every one o' ye."

"Can we hurry?" asked a young man in a baseball cap. He was holding some kind of Eastern-style dagger and awkwardly waving it back and forth. A green stalked him from six feet away.

The beast shook itself like a wet dog and released a furious bellow.

"Get inside," ordered Dale. "Yoo eejits have ballsed this right up."

Ryan turned to help Chloe and Fiona, but he found Helen blocking his way. She lifted her machete and swung it right at him. He could do nothing but scream. To his left, a green fell to the ground, its head half hanging off. Helen turned and hurried to the pub.

Miles came up behind Ryan and took his arm. "She just saved yer life, lad."

Ryan nodded, heart lodged in his throat. "Maybe she just wants to be the one to end me."

"Maybe. Now start running."

Everyone sprinted for safety. The pub's double doors were

hanging wide open. Dale stood in the entrance and slammed the left door shut. His expression was no less furious than when Helen had disobeyed him. He glared at Ryan.

A green came up on the left. Ryan put an arm out and directed Miles around it. "Look out."

Miles dodged aside. He was huffing and puffing. "I'm getting too old for this."

Ryan slowed down to help him, but when he reached out a hand, Miles flew upwards into the air. A bunch of blood-soaked talons exploded from his chest and lifted him higher. A breathless moan escaped his lips, along with a gout of thick red blood.

"Miles!"

The beast whipped around, launching Miles into the air. His punctured body landed amongst the greens and disappeared.

"Noooo!"

The beast glared at Ryan with its giant, pulsating eye. In that moment, it revealed its intelligence. It looked at Ryan in the same way Ryan was looking at it. With loathing.

You killed Miles, and one way or another, I'm going to kill you.

The beast charged at Ryan.

Ryan threw himself into a roll, avoiding its whipping talons, and then rose back to his feet. He sprinted for the pub's single open door.

Dale glared at him from the entrance, the shotgun hanging next to his leg.

The door began to close.

What? He's locking me out. Why?

Ryan ran as fast as his wounded foot would allow him, but the door was already halfway closed. He would never make it in time. He was going to end up stranded outside with the beast and Choirikell's former residents. "You bastard! Wait!"

Dale grinned. For some reason, the man hated him.

The door was about to close fully, but then it suddenly sprung back open. Cameron appeared in the entrance, drunkenly barging Dale aside. "English, get a feckin' leg on. Them bastards are right behind ye."

Ryan pumped his arms and legs, running faster than he ever had in his life. He made it through the door and Cameron bundled him inside, where he quickly collapsed onto the grungy carpet. He was panting so hard his chest hurt. Cameron helped him back to his feet and Ryan threw his arms around him.

After a moment, Cameron shoved him back. "Away, ye daft pillock."

Dale glared at Ryan in a mixture of shock and fury. He slammed the remaining door closed, locked it with a long brass key, and marched away. Seconds later, a dozen talons whipped against the other side of the wood. Bugs began to scurry beneath the door.

Everyone inside the pub panicked. They were under siege.

Helen marched to the doors and stared at Ryan. "Miles? Where's Miles?"

Ryan shook his head. "The beast... I'm sorry."

"What? No, we have to go an' help him. I can't shut him out again. I already let him down once."

"He's gone. I'm sorry. It happened so fast."

For the first time, Helen looked at Ryan with something other than hatred. She was devastated, just like she had been when her son had been taken from her. "I owed him," she muttered, then wandered away in a daze.

Cameron was stomping on bugs, but he stopped to shake his head. "The vicar is really gone? Feckin' hell."

"Ryan?" Fiona shouted from across the room. "We need to help Chloe."

"Yeah, right." He hurried across the room, passing by a dozen strangers. There were even more people left alive than he'd expected. Miles's death hadn't been in vain.

So why does it feel like such a waste?

I would be dead if not for him.

It's not my fault. Deal with it. Time to stop blaming myself.

Aaron and Tom were standing with Fiona. All three were fussing over Chloe. Blood gushed from a thick gash on the left side of her head, so deep that Ryan could see her skull. A few days ago, the sight would have made him vomit. Now, it was something he was used to. The strangers that he didn't know all kept their distance, sitting around at the various tables or keeping watch by the windows.

"We need to burn it out," said Fiona. "Like you did with my arm."

Ryan frowned. "How? Does this place have a boiler?"

"What are yoo feckers talking aboot?" demanded Dale. He had his shotgun levelled across his hip. Everyone in the group seemed to give him a wide berth. Some were trying to stack tables against the windows to keep the greens from getting inside.

Ryan was almost afraid to talk to the man, but he needed to help Chloe. "Does this place have a boiler? Or an oven that still lights?"

"Boiler's plumbed into the gas mains. It ain't worked for days. The oven neither."

Chloe sobbed. "I'm going to turn into one of them." Rifle fire outside made her flinch. "I'm so fecking screwed."

Aaron rubbed her back. "No you're not. We've got you, okay? You're going to be fine. I promise."

"She's done for," said Dale. "Nowt will change it."

"Shut the fuck up, Dale," said Fiona. "You don't know anything."

He took a step closer, threateningly, but Helen moved in his way. There were tears in her eyes, but she spoke firmly. "Try to help, Dale." She looked at Ryan. "We have matches, would that work?"

Ryan shrugged. "I dunno. Maybe."

"Bleach," said Tom. "We all saw the effect that bleach has on them."

"Bleach?" asked Helen. "What are you talking aboot?"

Aaron was nodding enthusiastically. "We used bleach on the

greens outside. It burns them. It kills them. We can use it to kill the fungus in Chloe's wound."

"It'll hurt like hell," said Dale.

"Better than being infected," said Aaron.

"Agreed," said Tom. "We need to try something."

Dale shrugged. "All right. Well, there's a tonne of the stuff in the kitchen. Industrial strength."

Helen moved. "I'll go fetch some. Ed, come help me."

The young lad in the baseball cap went after her.

"Hurry," said Fiona. She, too, had tears in her eyes. Miles had meant a great deal to a lot of people.

Chloe sobbed. Aaron gathered her into a hug and held her tightly.

Cameron limped over and patted Dale on the back. He was still clearly drunk, but was at least moving around under his own control. "Good to see ye alive, pal. I've got some stories to tell ye. Been stuck with the army, I have. Bloody fascists. Got a bullet in the arse from one of 'em."

Dale sniffed. "The army *is* here then? We thought as much. Killing anything that comes oot the village, I suspect."

As if to confirm it, more rifle fire clattered nearby.

"They helped a few," said Cameron. "Yoo made it on yer own, though, huh? Still a tough bastard, aye?"

Dale stared at Ryan as he answered. "Ye know me, Cameron Pollock. I dinnae take prisoners."

Ryan shuddered. He wanted to challenge the man about why he'd intended to close the door and leave him to die, but it felt like it would ignite things. Until he understood the situation better, Ryan didn't want to prod the bear holding a shotgun. "Thanks for rescuing us, Dale," he said cautiously. "I'm Ryan."

"Aye. Like I said, I've heard a lot aboot yoo English lads."

"What do you mean?"

"I've got it," said Helen, racing out from behind the bar, hefting a five-litre plastic bottle in her hand. "There's a dozen bottles of the stuff back there." Ed was right behind her, carrying two more bottles.

Dale nodded. "Health and hygiene. Get through a bottle of the stuff a day when we're open."

"Well, yer closed for now, pal," said Cameron.

Tom took the bleach from Helen and unscrewed the cap. He hesitated. "Do I just pour it on?"

Ryan shrugged. "Unless you have a better idea?"

"Just do it fast," said Fiona. "Before it spreads."

Tom swallowed. "It's going to hurt."

"It's okay," said Chloe, turning her head sideways so that her wound was accessible. Blood caked the side of her face, stained her blonde hair. "Get it over with. I don't want to die."

Aaron squeezed her hand. "You're going to be fine."

Chloe smiled at him. "If I were nae a lesbian..." She frowned. "Yer'd still be a wee lad, so best I dinnae finish that sentence."

Aaron chuckled, then repeated himself. "You're going to be fine."

Ryan gave Tom the nod, and he raised the heavy bottle of bleach. "Close your eyes and don't breathe," he said. He upended the bottle and a thick, acrid stream drenched Chloe's head and face. The fumes were so strong that Ryan's eyes watered and the back of his throat closed up. He had to turn away. Chloe spluttered and coughed.

"Make sure you get it all," said Fiona.

"This is stupid," said Dale. "Yer a bunch o' fools."

"It works," said Cameron. "Burns the greens like acid, it does."

"The opposite, actually," said Aaron. "Bleach is a strong alkaline. A high PH."

Cameron rolled his eyes but gave a small chuckle. "Whatever, little English."

Dale must have noticed the camaraderie, and he clearly disapproved. He sneered and went over to the bar. "Feckin' English."

Chloe hissed and tried to speak between splutters. "It-It hurts."

Fiona rubbed her back. "I know, hun."

"It's almost over," said Aaron.

"Get it off me!"

"Just a little longer."

"GET IT OFF ME!" Chloe leapt up out of the chair and shoved Aaron so fiercely that he went sprawling onto the ground. Fiona tried to grab her and calm her down, but she lashed out and backhanded her in the face. Ryan caught her, keeping her on her feet.

"The stupid cow's gunna attract the greens," said Dale. "Tell her to keep quiet."

"They already know we're in here," said Aaron, clambering up off the floor. "What planet are you on?"

Fiona pushed herself out of Ryan's arms and tried to grab Chloe again, but she was lashing out so frantically, and screaming so madly, that it was impossible to get close. She was in agony – way more than she should have been. Something was wrong. The rifle fire outside only added to the chaos.

And what's that smell?

Petrol?

Ryan threw himself at Chloe, tackling her around the arms and holding her in place. He tried to get her attention, but she was a wild horse. Bleach and blood dripped down her face. Green ooze pulsed beneath her cheek near her ears. Black threads ran down towards her jaw and sideways towards her eye. She began to convulse, her body flip-flopping. Her jaw clamped shut. The tip of her tongue hung on her chin, attached by a single bloody sinew. Then her eyes rolled back in her head and she tilted like a peg, toppling onto the ground. There, she convulsed even harder, blood and foam erupting from her mouth. Her cheek split wide open, revealing a great mass of fizzing green oil.

Less than a minute later, Chloe was dead.

Fiona covered her mouth with a hand and began shaking. "No. No, she can't be dead. We... we were trying to help her."

Aaron looked like he was about to throw up. "The bleach killed the fungus, but the reaction was too... too severe. It killed her too. She's gone." He turned and kicked a chair with more ferocity than Ryan had ever seen from him. "Goddamn it!" Ryan went and held him, but his brother pushed him away. "She was my fucking friend, man."

"I know. I get it."

Helen sat down on a chair and put her head in her hands. "This is pointless. It doesn't matter what we do. We're all gonna end up the same way."

"That's not true," said Ryan. "We've been worried about you, Helen. We feared the worst, but here you are, still alive. We can get out of this." He looked around the room at the faces, both familiar and foreign. "The army is leaving here tomorrow, and we need to make sure we go with them."

Dale spat. "None of us here is aboot to walk into a firing squad. We were heading for the hills when yoo eejits appeared and fecked everything up. Not fer the first time, either, from what I hear."

"We came to warn you all," said Ryan. "The army is going to set fire to the village. And what fucking problem do you have with me? You tried to lock me outside."

Dale took a step towards him, the shotgun raised slightly in his arms.

A window cracked.

One of the people Ryan didn't know raced over to shove a table up against the gap. A stream of bugs began to fall from the windowsills.

"We need to get the feck oota here," said Dale, lifting his shotgun and firing it at the broken window. He narrowly missed taking out the person standing there.

"We can leave through the back," said a woman with a deep tan and sun-weathered skin.

Helen nodded. "Come on."

Everyone got moving. The strangers from the pub picked up various bags and holdalls, along with deadly looking knives and machetes. "Any extra?" asked Ryan.

"Not fer the likes of yoo," said Dale. "Maybe I'll show ye my antique tanto blade later if I get the chance."

It was a clear threat, but Ryan tried to act like he hadn't realised. Antagonising the man was not a smart move right now. "So, this is *your* pub, huh?" he asked as they hurried behind the bar.

"Aye, and it were a fortress until yoo came along. Just like the church and the bowls club. Seems like everywhere ye go, people die."

Ryan instinctively hated this man, and wanted to argue, but there was too much guilt weighing down on him to try. The man had only said things he had already been thinking. "Things were bad at the church. Helen's son…"

Dale stopped walking and turned to him. "*My* son."

Ryan skidded to avoid colliding with the man. He gasped. "Andy was your son? I-I'm sorry."

"Aye. Ye will be."

Ryan let the man carry on ahead. Aaron and Cameron were just behind, and they both caught up to Ryan at the same time. "Dale's a right hard nut," said Cameron, almost seeming to marvel. "Nae surprise he's been kicking arse this whole time."

Ryan nodded. "He's dangerous?"

"As dangerous as they come. Watch yerself around him, English. Dale nae likes strangers."

"Yeah, I'm getting that. I think he tried to kill me."

Cameron frowned at Ryan in a mixture of humour and concern. "He did what now?"

Ryan went to explain, but more windows in the pub shattered and prompted them to pick up the pace. Greens appeared everywhere outside, blocking out the light. There was no time to dawdle. "Nothing. Don't worry about it."

Cameron nodded, then limped along to catch up to the others. It left Ryan and Aaron alone behind the bar.

"That Dale seems like bad news," said Aaron.

"He is," said Ryan, "and he wants me dead."

"Why?"

"Because he's Andy's dad."

Aaron's face fell as he realised, like Ryan already had, that the pub was not a safe place. In fact, they were in even more danger than ever.

THE PUB'S kitchen was surprisingly vast and modern, in contrast to the old carpets and dark wood of the bar. The counters were shaped from gleaming stainless steel, and every utensil was in its proper place. Dale kept a clean establishment.

Ryan kept to the rear of the group with Aaron. He wanted to make sure he could keep an eye on Dale, and the shotgun he was holding. For now the man's attention was on getting everyone gathered at the centre of the kitchen where there was a large square island.

He blames me for Andy's death.

Helen told him it was my fault.

No wonder he wants to kill me.

Helen and the young lad in the baseball cap started heaving industrial bottles of bleach onto a large central island. The containers clearly weighed a lot, because they both grunted with each one they hoisted off the ground.

"We won't be able to make use of them like this," said Fiona. "They're too heavy."

"Do we have any smaller containers?" asked Tom.

Cameron grabbed a bottle and held it by his hip. He wielded it far more easily than the women had. Even with a bullet lodged in his arse. "I can manage just fine."

"The rest of us aren't so fucking strong," Fiona yelled. It made Cameron flinch.

"Yeah, all right, lass. Keep yer knickers on."

Fiona's face cracked. She was holding back sobs. She looked away and held up a hand to Cameron. "I'm sorry. It's just... Chloe and Miles."

Cameron nodded. "I know, sweetheart. They were good people."

Helen sighed. "I never really knew Chloe, but Miles helped me get out of a pretty bad situation once." Her eyes flicked briefly to Dale. "He helped a lot of people in Choirikell."

"He helped me too," said Fiona. "Anyway, as I was saying. These bleach bottles are too heavy."

"Empty them," said Aaron. "Just a little, until they're light enough."

"We can't waste any of it," said Tom. "This stuff is the only way we have of fighting back."

Helen looked around. "Here!" She grabbed a steel mop bucket on wheels, then a bottle of bleach. "Pour the excess in here. We can take it with us."

Everyone grabbed a bottle and tipped a third away until the mop bucket was full. They only managed to lighten four or five bottles. Not enough for the entire group.

"We need a plan B," said Aaron.

Dale was leaning over the central island, a permanent scowl on his face. "There's bottled water in the pantry. Ye could pour some of it into those."

"Good thinking." Cameron put down the bleach and limped over to a small doorway at the edge of the kitchen. He yanked it open to reveal a narrow space full of shelving. The pantry was well-stocked with crates of ingredients and packaged snacks. "Feck me! What happened here?"

Ryan sidestepped so that he could see what Cameron was looking at. There, at his feet, was a body. Bloody and mangled.

"Who is that?" Fiona asked.

"Oliver," said the lad in the baseball cap sadly.

"He didn't play by ma rules," said Dale.

For a moment, Ryan thought the man was joking, but then he saw the timid expressions on the faces of the strangers. Dale had killed this man.

Cameron grimaced. "Oliver Threadwell? I nae liked the guy, but hell, no one should end up like this."

"Can yer just grab the water bottles?" said Dale testily. "We need to get a move on."

"Aye, all right, pal." Cameron grabbed a pack of one-litre water bottles wrapped together in plastic and plonked it down on the centre island. He stepped away, gritting his teeth in pain and putting a hand against his bandaged buttock.

"Empty the bottles," Dale ordered everyone. "Move it."

Everyone rushed into action, grabbing the bottles of water and drinking from them, then spilling whatever they couldn't stomach. Once they had a dozen empty bottles, Cameron and Dale started filling them from the large bottles of bleach.

There was gunfire outside, a constant drone of it from within the village.

Back in the bar, tables and chairs tipped over and made a racket. The greens were inside the pub.

Dale yelled at the lad in the cap. "Ed, get that feckin' door barricaded before they get in here."

Ed leapt to attention and hurried over to the door that led back behind the bar. There was a stainless steel serving trolley to the left of it, so he wheeled it in front of the door and kicked on the brake. Then he grabbed a large microwave from the corner and hefted it on top of the trolley. It wouldn't hold for long, but it put some weight between them and the door. The door at the opposite end of the kitchen must have been their exit.

Everyone in the group now had a bottle of bleach in their hands, except for Dale, who kept his shotgun. The sounds coming from the bar, and the gunfire outside, were worrying, yet Ryan felt oddly confident. They had found a way to hurt the greens, and there were now more than a dozen of them ready to fight back. Perhaps it was finally time to stop running.

"Are we ready?" Dale asked.

Ryan nodded. "The army's camp is only a few hundred metres from the edge of the village. If we stick together and keep moving, we can get there."

"The fuck asked fer yer advice, English?"

Cameron put a hand up. "Easy, Dale. He's all right."

"He ain't fecking all right with me."

Fiona frowned. "What's your problem with Ryan? Whatever it is, you think maybe you can put it to one side while we try not to die?"

Dale smirked. "Nae problem here, sweetheart."

There was a thud against the door that led to the bar. The trolley skidded aside. Ed panicked, throwing his shoulder against it and trying to shove it back. "It's nae heavy enough. We need to go."

Dale put a hand on the arm of the woman with saggy tanned skin. "Get the back door, Shel."

The woman hurried across the kitchen without argument. People moved with her, bunching up in a group while she grabbed the deadbolt on the back door and turned it. "Ready?"

"Aye," said Dale, aiming his shotgun at the door. "Open it."

Shel opened the door to a sea of green. There were infected people everywhere.

Dale fired his shotgun, narrowly missing his companions gathered at the door. Luckily, Shel had already leapt back in fright. The greens in the doorway flew backwards, several of them hit by the buckshot. Others soon stepped in to take their place.

"Close the door," Tom shouted. "Close it!"

Shel slammed the door again, and the deadbolt clacked shut. At the other end of the kitchen, the trolley was skidding once again. Ed sprinted over to go and shove it back again. This time, others rushed to help him.

"We're trapped," said Dale. "I feckin' told ye this would

happen. Ye dragged us back inside to help that girl, and she's dead anyway."

"We had no choice," said Fiona.

"We did, and now we're all fecked." Dale strode back and forth for a moment, and then he shocked everyone by levelling his shotgun at Ryan. "Ye're a feckin' demon. Ye brought a plague doon on this place, and yer'll nae be happy until we're all dead."

Ryan put his hands up. "Whoa, man. This thing has nothing to do with me. When we make it to the army camp, you can speak to Lieutenant Holloway yourself. This is some kind of attack."

"Or aliens," said Cameron, nodding at Aaron. A few of the strangers from the pub chuckled.

Dale kept the shotgun aimed at Ryan, but he turned his head to sneer at Cameron. "Have ye lost yer heid? Never thought I'd see you standing up for a bunch of feckin' English."

Cameron shrugged. "Just tryna stay alive, pal. We need to work through this together."

"No," said Dale. "Everyone needs to do exactly what they're feckin' told. This is ma pub and I'm the boss."

"Easy to say that when you're holding a shotgun," said Tom.

Dale turned the shotgun on him. "Ye think ye could take me otherwise, do ye? All right, Lord English. How 'boot I put this doon and yoo and me can see who's got the biggest nuts."

Tom shrunk back a step and put up a shaking hand. "I'm not suggesting we do anything of the sort, but waving a shotgun in people's faces isn't exactly helpful, is it?"

"I disagree." Dale pointed the shotgun back at Ryan. "Ye see, this foul bag o' shite killed ma wee boy. Because of him, poor Helen had to watch her sweet, innocent tulip die."

Aaron shook his head. "What are you talking about?"

"Andy! I'm talking about ma boy. He's dead because of ye English bastards. Now, it's time to pay." He glared at Ryan. "Say goodnight, ye sonofabitch."

"Wait," Tom called out. Aaron yelled something incomprehensible.

Ryan knew right then and there that Dale was about to pull the trigger and blow his brains out, but somehow Tom managed to stop it from happening. He threw himself against Dale and knocked him against the central island. The shotgun clattered against the stainless steel surface, but Dale managed to keep hold of it, even as Tom rained down punches on his face.

The problem was that Tom was no fighter. Never had been. His punches were like flies landing, and Dale quickly shoved him away from him and managed to stand up straight. He lifted the shotgun and rammed the stock at Tom's face. Tom sprawled backwards against a double oven, taking the impact with his hip and tumbling to the ground. He held his face in both hands and squealed as Dale pivoted and aimed the shotgun at him.

Dale snarled. "Nice try, but no cigar."

Tom put up a blood-covered hand. "Please, don't."

"Only dead men beg. Close yer eyes. I'm gunna switch ye off, pal."

Aaron leapt at Dale, having grabbed a cast-iron skillet from somewhere. It clonked off Dale's skull with a dull thud and sent the man cross-eyed. He staggered back against the countertops, using them to keep himself upright. Somehow, he still managed to keep a hold of his shotgun.

Cameron moved to intervene, grabbing at the shotgun and trying to wrench it from Dale's hand. Recovering from his daze, Dale headbutted Cameron in the face and sent him reeling. Cameron then seemed to remember that he had a pistol in his waistband, but when he grabbed for it, he fumbled and it went skating across the tiles. "Shit on it!"

Aaron leapt in with the frying pan again, but this time Dale sidestepped and struck him with a vicious elbow. As Aaron staggered away, Dale raised the shotgun and prodded the muzzle against his chest. "Ye little fecker!"

Ryan had been standing frozen, stunned by the sudden brawl, but now his brother was in danger and his body sparked with electricity. He threw himself around the centre aisle. "Aaron!"

A blast erupted, echoing off the gleaming steel worktops and the rigid floor tiles. The stench of bleach gave way to something smokier.

All the colour left Ryan's vision.

He felt light. So light that he could've flown if he'd tried. His body no longer existed, only a numbness that seemed to spread from the centre of his mind. He looked down, almost like he was watching himself in a daydream, and saw blood. Blood everywhere. All over him. His stomach was leaking the stuff.

Aaron's hands were on him, holding him tightly and lowering him gently down to the floor.

Or am I falling?

The back of Ryan's head thudded against the floor tiles, and suddenly he was looking up at the ceiling. At the mortified faces of his friends: Fiona, Tom, Cameron.

Aaron.

Aaron's here. He's okay.

We're all going to be fine.

AARON LOOKED DOWN at his brother in disbelief. Hot blood was everywhere. All over his hands. All over his brother. It gushed out of Ryan's stomach.

That bastard shot him.

Aaron leapt up to face the monster in the room. Dale still held the smoking shotgun against his shoulder. He didn't seem in the least shocked by what he had done. This wasn't his first kill. "What the hell have you done? You shot my fucking brother."

"Don't worry, lad, yer aboot to join him."

Aaron knew it was stupid, but he rushed to attack Dale again. This time he didn't even have the skillet. He only managed to get one punch in before Dale shoved him back against the counter and levelled the shotgun at his face. Aaron froze, staring into the black hole at the end of the barrel. "Just do it. Get it fucking over with!"

Dale scowled. "Why make it fast when we can make it slow?" He turned the shotgun around and rammed the stock into Aaron's ribs. A wail burst from his lungs and he couldn't breathe. He sprawled against the centre island, panicking and trying to suck in air. Dale struck him again, this time in the side of the head. Pain spiked through his ear and his vision darkened. He tumbled off the countertop and landed on his knees. He tried to crawl away across the cold, hard tiles.

"Fecking stop this, Dale," Cameron shouted from somewhere. "This has got oota hand. I'll feckin shoot yer dead, ye mad cunt."

"Leave him alone," Tom shouted weakly. "I'll kill you."

People in the kitchen were screaming, crying out for mercy.

They don't want to watch me die, thought Aaron. *I'm just a kid. I don't want to die.*

Aaron was still yet to take a breath. He was dizzy – sick – and he knew he was on the edge of passing out. It was like being on a rollercoaster, but the drop seemed to go on forever.

"All right, fine," Dale shouted. "Let's get this over with."

"Dinnae do it," said Cameron. He had regained his pistol and was aiming it at Dale's head. "I nae want to shoot a pal."

"Then don't. This is between me and the boy."

Aaron found half a breath, sucking in a whimper of air. He rolled onto his back and looked up to see the shotgun pointed at his face. Behind it was the hate-filled monster about to murder him.

I don't even know this man. I don't even know him and he's about to kill me.

Dale flinched, and so did Aaron. Aaron thought he had pulled the trigger, but nothing happened. Something else had caused him to twitch suddenly.

Helen had appeared at Dale's side. Her eyes were filled with as much rage and hatred as his, but there was something else there too. Compassion? Humanity?

Dale dropped the shotgun on the tiles and staggered backwards into the counter behind him. His hand went to his side where a large rubber handle hovered between his ribs. Helen had buried her machete right inside his chest cavity. There was hardly any blood, but Dale's eyes were already fading, turning from glossy to matte.

"He was ma daffodil," said Helen. "Not ma tulip. If ye'd ever been around for him, ye woulda known that."

Dale's final expression was one of confusion. He really didn't seem to understand what was happening, and before he got anywhere close to an answer, Cameron stepped forward and shot him in the face. His expression afterwards was pained, already haunted by what he had done. He turned to Helen. "I finished him off, lass. This was nae on yoo."

Helen closed her eyes, took a breath, then bent down and picked up Dale's fallen shotgun. "He was already dead and ye know it. A mercy killing was all it was. I'm the one who took his life." She turned and spat on Dale's corpse. "And I'm fine wi' it."

Noise seemed to assault the kitchen from all sides. The greens beat at the doors, front and back. People in the room gasped and wept.

Aaron gasped, finally finding the ability to breathe again.

Tom crawled over to him on the tiles and gathered him into a hug.

"English?" Cameron limped around the counter and dropped to the floor next to Ryan. "English, ye gotta stay with us, eh? Stay with us!"

Aaron realised his brother was still alive.

He's still here. He's still here.

Ryan had managed to drag himself up against a cabinet, where he was now sitting, peering around sleepily. His entire mid-section was drenched in blood, but he made no attempts to ease his wounds. His hands lay limply by his sides. Cameron pinched at his cheeks, trying to rouse him.

"Will you... stop that," Ryan muttered. "You mad Scottish bastard."

Cameron chuckled. "Just making sure ye're still with us, lad. We're gunna sort ye oot, okay?"

Tom and Aaron dragged themselves along the blood-spattered tiles to join them. Fiona came over as well. Together, they formed a semicircle around Ryan while the others in the kitchen gave them some room. The greens attacking the doors no longer mattered. Barely background noise.

Fiona got on her knees and hugged Ryan. "You're not allowed to die. You've got places to be, things to do."

Ryan nodded. "Always thought I was born to die in Manchester. Whoever thought I'd die in a foreign country."

"You're not going to die. I'm not going to let you."

"Thanks."

"Thank me later, over a bottle of vodka."

"I thought you quit drinking."

She chuckled. "Irn-Bru then."

Aaron was still catching his breath, but he couldn't sit by and say nothing. His voice was thin and reedy, but he forced out his words. "We've got to get back home, Ryan. You and me. You promised."

Ryan managed a tiny smile. "I promised *you* would see home again. Think it might be a bit of a stretch for me now."

"No! No, I can't make it without you. There's no way."

"You *will* make it because you'll have help." Ryan glanced sideways, looking at Cameron. "Fancy taking on a little brother?"

Cameron frowned, but then his face grew as serious as a stone wall. "Aye, I reckon I do."

"Even an English one?"

"I'll teach him to drink and swear like a true Scot."

"And fight," said Ryan. "Make him a fighter, like you."

Cameron nodded. There were tears in his eyes. "Aye, pal, ye have ma word."

"Aaron will have me, too," said Tom. "I let you down, Ryan –

I'm so sorry – but I promise I'll get Aaron home safe. Atonement, right?"

Ryan nodded weakly. "You go find Amanda and never let her go, okay?"

Tom nodded. "You have my word. I'll make an honest woman of her."

Ryan turned to Fiona, his movements heavy and slow. "Y-You're... family now. Aaron's your responsibility, whether you want him... or not."

Tears streamed down her cheeks, but she managed a laugh between sobs. "I want him."

"Good. One last thing."

"What?"

"What's with your manky earlobe?"

Fiona laughed, wiping away snot with the back of her hand. "A stick."

"A... stick?"

"Yeah. When I was a little girl, I was running around with this stick I found. Slipped over and it went right through my earlobe. The scarring kept it from growing properly."

"Oh, I thought it would be... something cooler."

"Sorry to disappoint."

Aaron was shaking his head. All these people were talking about him, but he didn't want to hear it. They were focusing on the wrong thing. "Ryan, stop talking like this. We're going to get you back to camp. The army can get you all patched up."

"Even if the doc was still around," Ryan whispered, "it wouldn't make a difference." He lifted up his jumper, revealing a mass of torn and bleeding flesh. Aaron couldn't even make out what he was seeing. It was liked mashed potato mixed with tomato juice.

Ryan's last meal. Potato and baked beans.

This isn't happening.

Aaron was still shaking his head. "You need to live, do you hear me? What about Sophie?"

Ryan's head was starting to hang. "I-I need to you to make it home for me, little brother. You find Mum and you look after her. Then you find Sophie and..."

"Ryan?" Aaron panicked. He grabbed his brother and shook him. "Ryan, wake up!"

Ryan opened his eyes again and managed to lift his head a little. He looked Aaron in the eyes and spoke a little louder. "Find Sophie. Tell her... I never had a future until the day I met her. That I never felt my heart beat... until... until the moment she first looked at me. Tell her I did my best... to get back to her. Tell her I tried. I did."

Aaron nodded. "You need to *keep* trying."

Ryan shook his head. "Be better than me, little brother. Be the man I was never able to be. Be brave. Be... Be..." He took a gulp of air and his eyes suddenly seemed to lose focus. He no longer saw Aaron, he was seeing something else. "*Ant Man 2.*"

"What?"

"Did he just say *Ant Man 2*?" asked Cameron.

Aaron watched his brother's chin fall onto his chest and a thin line of bloody drool escape his lips. This time, he didn't try and wake him up again. Ryan was gone. His brother was dead. It felt like a rib breaking in his chest – a sudden snap of agonising, breathtaking pain.

Cameron reached down and placed a hand on Aaron's shoulder, but he didn't say anything.

"Ye all need to go," said Helen. She had moved over to the door that led to the bar. There, Ed and the other people Aaron didn't know were lending their weight, trying to keep the greens from getting in.

"How?" asked Fiona. "We're surrounded."

"Ye've got the bleach, right? Yer gonna have to fight yer way oot."

"Aren't you coming with us?"

She held up the shotgun, but her expression remained blank. "Think I'll stay here and put ma feet up. I'm tired. Too tired."

"We're not leaving ye here alone," said Cameron.

"Then stay. I dinnae much care. Either way, I say you have about two minutes to make up your mind."

Cameron was shaking his head. "Helen..."

Ed squealed by the door. The trolley was slowly skidding on the tiles. "They're getting through."

Aaron got to his feet. His ribs creaked and his breathing stuttered, but he was okay.

No, I'm not okay. Not even close.

I'm alive, and that's all.

"I'm not going to die here in this goddamn kitchen," he said, and he crouched down next to his brother. He reached inside Ryan's jean pocket, rooting around. Touching his brother's cooling flesh was strange, like prodding a piece of clay. It was no longer him.

"What are you doing?" asked Tom, scrunching up his nose.

Aaron found what he was looking for. He held the folded sheet of paper up for everyone to see. "I won't let my brother's final words be *Ant Man 2*. He wrote a letter. I need to deliver it." He stood back up. "Let's get the fuck out of here. I'm going home."

8

Despite being in a dire situation, no one complained. Perhaps it was because they had no other choice, or maybe it was due to the amount of death they had witnessed during the last hour. Everyone grabbed as much bottled bleach as they could carry, while the young lad, Ed, picked up a pair of the large bottles, offering to be Cameron's bleach caddie.

Miles, Chloe, Ryan.

And the bastard who killed him.

Why did Helen stab him? Didn't she hate me and my brother?

Ryan's dead. It... It just doesn't make sense.

He can't be gone.

Aaron had to get out of his own head. He grabbed a water bottle of bleach from the countertop and shoved a second one inside the waistband of his jeans. Then he knelt beside Ryan, realising these were the last moments he would ever get with his brother.

"Thanks for always giving a shit, Ryan, no matter how different we were, or how much I disappointed you. You never stopped trying to be there for me. I wish I'd made the same effort for you. I love you, man. I'm gunna miss you." He stood up and went over to the centre island, leaning over it and wondering if he were going to be sick.

"Sorry aboot yer brother," said the middle-aged woman with tanned skin. "I'm Shel."

Aaron nodded, the woman's words barely registering. "Aaron."

"It's nice to meet ye, Aaron." She walked away.

"Once that door opens," Cameron shouted, now appearing completely sober, "we need to get oot and spread oot. If them bastards get us all bunched together, we'll nae make it out of here."

"I'll get the door," said Tom. There was a noticeable change to him. His expression was hard, his polite manner broken. No longer did he seem like someone who was willing to sit back and let others take the lead. He was angry.

Aaron glanced about in a daze, taking in the unfamiliar faces of his new companions. He saw a mixture of fear and courage, youth and age. It made him realise, perhaps for the first time, that the world, and not just Choirikell, was full of frightened people now having to fight for their lives. How many brothers, sons, and daughters had been lost? How many grieving souls were currently feeling what he was feeling? Angry. Empty. Desperate. He saw all of those things in Helen, but only now did he truly understand them. He moved over to her and attempted a smile, but he couldn't manage it. She was leaning up against a counter, showing little interest in anything that was going on. "Are you really not coming with us?"

She flinched, then looked at Aaron as if he had just spoken a foreign language. There was dried blood on her palms and she scratched at it with her nails. Dale's shotgun was propped against her leg. "There's nowhere I need to be, so I might as well stay here."

"I'm sorry."

She grunted. "For what?"

Aaron shrugged. "I'm just sorry."

"Yeah, me too, I suppose."

"You should come with us."

"Just go."

Aaron was unwilling to argue, it was her choice, so he turned around just in time to see Tom readying himself at the door. Cameron was behind him with a five-litre bottle of bleach held high. At the other end of the kitchen, Ed and the others were pressed up against the trolley, ready to spring away from the barricade and run across the kitchen as soon as the door opened.

"Okay," said Tom. "After three. One... Two... Three! Shit!"

Cameron groaned. "Ye gotta turn the bolt, yer daft shite."

"Sorry! Okay, here goes." Tom turned the bolt and yanked open the door. He quickly stood aside so that Cameron could unleash a thick stream of bleach that drenched the greens standing outside the doorway. They started to burn. A talon lashed out and struck the doorframe. Squeals erupted, joining in with the distant gunfire. A cacophony of war.

"The army's nearby," said Fiona. "We should try and join up with them."

Cameron unleashed another stream of bleach, burning another bunch of greens. "Ye heard what that corporal said. They'll shoot us if we try to go back."

"We'll have to take our chances," said Aaron. He moved beside Cameron and thrust out his water bottle. The bleach landed on an infected woman with one giant breast hanging loose from a black halter top. The green immediately let out a squeal and started to convulse. Black smoke spiralled from its naked breast. Flesh burning.

Cameron booted the infected woman in the chest and her breast popped like a giant oozing zit. She went reeling backwards into those behind her and disappeared in the crowd.

"Her feckin' titty popped," said Cameron. "Can ye believe it?"

"I believe a lot of things," said Tom, grimacing.

Cameron hopped through the doorway and unleashed another torrent of bleach. Aaron saw a gap open up behind him and moved into it. More greens squealed as their flesh burned. They fell to the ground one after the other.

The pub's survivors piled out of the doorway, battling to spread out, pushing back the greens with multiple arcing streams of bleach. The air filled with the stench of charred alien flesh.

Eventually, everyone made it out of the kitchen and stood on the patio behind the pub. Then the true horror made itself known. The pub's beer garden was packed with greens, countless talons whipping at the air. The village's residents stood in front of them, all infected. All murderous.

"Dinnae waste a drop," said Cameron, flicking another pint of bleach into the air.

"Over here," shouted Tom. "There's a way through."

The group turned as a single organism, strangers and friends quickly finding a way to work together. Everyone flicked their bottles, creating a three-hundred-and-sixty-degree aura of destruction. They followed Tom as he led the way around the side of the pub. There was no end to the greens in sight, but they kept on going, managing to keep the enemy at bay. They rounded the corner. The post office and car park came into view. In the other direction lay houses, cottages, and the petrol station. Beyond that, the half-dismantled army camp. Possible salvation, or maybe just a bullet in the head.

"Ah shite," said Cameron. "The road is thick with the bastards."

Aaron could see no way past. The edge of the village was completely blocked off by greens.

"Maybe we should try to head around the village," said Tom. "Skirt them."

"Aye," said Cameron. "Everyone get to the car park. We'll try the post office. Maybe we can go through the staff area around the back and give these bastards the runaround."

Everyone moved deeper into the village. It was the opposite of what they wanted, but they had no choice. The greens were sparser around the car park and presented the only way forward.

Perhaps the enemy had known that they would try to make a run for the petrol station.

They can think. Plan.

The greens behind them gave chase, leaving no choice but to continue onward. The greens that had made it inside the pub were now starting to clamber back through the windows and out of the busted-open double doors. Rather than wait to be attacked, Aaron edged towards the closest green and flicked bleach at its face. He enjoyed the sound of it squealing as its malformed green eye began to bubble and smoke, and then it popped open like a Cadbury's Creme Egg. He flicked his wrist again, and again, revelling in the destruction of flesh. He wanted to kill every last one of these motherfuckers. He flicked again. Again. He flicked bleach at a child.

Jesus.

The young boy was less covered by fuzz than the rest of the greens, and Aaron wondered if that meant the child had been infected more recently, yet to fully succumb to the alien fungus. The bleach he had just flicked missed its target, and the child was now approaching quickly. It raised a pair of thin tendrils into the air.

Aaron flicked the bottle again, forced to defend himself.

It was empty.

"Fook it!" He threw the empty bottle down and grabbed for the second in his waistband, but as he yanked it out, it caught awkwardly on his jumper and tumbled out of his hands. It landed on his foot and rolled away. "Double fook it!"

The child whipped its talons at Aaron.

Cameron pulled him aside just in time, then upended his five-litre jug of bleach over the child's head – emptying the last dregs left inside. The child let out an ear-piercing screech and began to thrash. A moment later it was dead.

Cameron turned and glared at Aaron. "Yoo dare get yerself killed less than an hour after I promised to keep ye safe."

"Sorry."

"Come on," said Tom. "We have to keep moving."

Everyone hurried for the car park. Ed handed one of the spare five-litre bleach bottles to Cameron, who opened the cap and got to work on the next group of greens. They were starting to thin out, most of their number behind instead of up front. Ahead, Aaron spotted Ryan's Audi. The journey they had taken in it seemed like a lifetime ago now. They had sat in silence most the way, with little to say and even less in common. Now, Aaron would do anything to be able to talk to his brother again.

The Audi was covered in green fuzz. It began to move.

What the...?

Aaron didn't understand what he was seeing. The Audi's tyres were skidding across the tarmac, spitting up gravel. The chassis was rocking back and forth on its suspension.

Then the tyres left the road, rose up into the air.

Aaron shouted. "Get down!"

The beast emerged from the shadow of the post office, its thick tendrils wrapped beneath the Audi, lofting it into the air as if it were a Hot Wheels car. It sailed through the air, right towards Aaron and the others. Before anyone could realise what was happening, blood had been spilled. The young lad, Ed, threw himself to the ground, baseball cap falling from his head to reveal thick blonde hair. Behind him stood the woman with the deep tan. The car went right through her, colliding with the road behind where she'd been standing. Her mangled body disappeared beneath the bouncing chassis. She didn't even get time to scream. Half a dozen greens were pinned beneath the wreckage as well, their talons whipping futilely as they fought to get free.

Ed clambered off the ground and looked back. "Shell! No!"

Helen grabbed the lad by the arm. "She's gone. Keep moving."

But they *couldn't* keep moving. Behind them was a legion of greens. Ahead was something worse.

The beast had grown again. Now, instead of a lumbering rhino, it was a giant squid. A bulbous head and shoulders tapered down into a snarl of talon-tipped tendrils. Rather than run towards them, it seemed to swish, propelling itself forward with pulsating thrusts. More disembodied skulls hung from its torso. It gathered bodies like the Grim Reaper himself.

Is this what we're fighting against? Is this our real enemy?

Is this an alien?

Aaron was without a bottle of bleach, having dropped his backup, so he had no choice but to stay close to Cameron. Doing what none of the rest of them could do, he wielded the large bottle of bleach as if it were a bottle of champagne on a Formula One podium. He flicked it left and right, taking care of the greens in their way, but there were bigger threats to worry about.

"It's too big," shouted Ed. He had dropped his remaining five-litre bottle and it was nowhere in sight. "And there are too many greens. We need to run."

As if it heard them, the beast swished sideways, blocking off the alleyway that ran behind Chloe's house. They could try and make it around the post office, but it would likely move to block them in that direction too.

"We need to head back," said Tom. "We can't fight that thing."

"There are too many behind us," said Fiona.

They were surrounded.

The beast propelled itself across the tarmac towards them.

Cameron leapt ahead of the group and upended his bottle of bleach, pouring it all over the ground.

Aaron shook his head. "What are you doing?"

"Buying us some time."

The beast picked up speed, but when it crossed over the puddle of bleach, it skidded to a halt, letting out a bellow far deeper than the pained squeals of its underlings. It began to smoke. A hundred tendrils lashed out at the sky in pain.

"Yoo hurt it," said Ed excitedly. "Yoo hurt it."

Cameron glared at the beast. "Every man dies, but not every man truly lives."

He may have expected a cheer, but no one said anything. They were too in awe of the gigantic, grotesque creature bellowing in front of them. Beneath the thick green fuzz was a translucent bulk like a sea creature, or a cancer. The beast was the complete opposite of anything human. It continued to thrash, but slowly its bellows faded. It seemed to glare back at Cameron with its one giant eye.

"It's recovering," said Tom. "We need to go."

Everyone turned back, but a hundred greens stood in their way. They could try to fight their way through, but the beast would be at them again soon. Eventually it would recover enough to whip them all to pieces.

A loud *slam* echoed off the pub's stone walls as its broken front doors burst open wide.

Helen emerged in the entrance, holding Dale's shotgun and rolling the steel mop bucket along in front of her. Her gaze briefly connected with Aaron's and he she gave a tiny nod. Then she gave the mop bucket a hefty kick and sent it careening across the pavement on its casters. It hit the bunched-up tendrils dragging behind the beast and flipped over, spilling ten litres of bleach all over the creature's rear. This time, the beast's bellow caused the ground to shake.

Everyone covered their ears.

The greens went into seizures, sharing in their master's agony.

Cameron's mouth fell open in a gasp. "Helen-lass?"

"Changed my mind." Her upper lip curled up in a snarl. "I've got some scores to settle." She lifted Dale's shotgun and pointed it at the beast's giant fuzzy eyeball. Then she pulled the trigger.

THE BEAST'S giant green eye exploded, sending fleshy spores into the air. Instinctively, Aaron covered his mouth with an arm, and he watched as the massive creature rose up, then tumbled backwards. Its talons sliced through the air, cutting apart a dozen nearby greens. One of the survivors from the pub got caught on the arm, an older gentleman, and he fell to the pavement in agony, blood gushing from his open wrist. The young lad, Ed, tried to help him, but a pair of greens closed in on him and prevented him from getting near.

Helen cracked the shotgun and pushed in a new pair of cartridges. Then she took aim and fired at the beast again. This time, the shotgun blasted its exposed belly, opening up a massive wet hole that immediately swarmed with bugs. She fired a third time, making the hole even bigger. Then she threw the shotgun on the ground and marched over to the others.

Aaron frowned at her. "What changed your mind?"

"I'm getting ye home to yer mother."

"What? Why? Why would you help me after what happened to your—"

"I'm nae doing it for yoo. I'm doing it for yer mother. She's already lost yer brother. She's nae gunna lose yoo too."

Cameron managed a thin smile. "I'm glad yer with us, Helen-lass, but we need to get oota here fast. If the greens dinnae get us, the army will."

Aaron realised that the army's rifle fire had got nearer. It sounded like they were waging war right around the corner. "They've avoided coming into the village all week. Why are they entering it now?"

"They're cleaning up before they go," said Fiona.

Tom sniffed at the air. "Do any of you smell that?"

Cameron narrowed his eyes and sniffed at the air. "Petrol?"

"Yes. I smelt it earlier in the pub, but it was much fainter."

Aaron's eyes went wide. "They're setting fire to the village."

Cameron growled. "They said we had until morning. The lying feckers."

"Um, guys," Fiona called out. She was standing with Ed and the rest of the survivors from the pub. "Can we be somewhere else, please?"

The greens were starting to close in. Some had split off and were heading towards the rifle fire, but dozens more were shambling towards the post office car park.

Helen sneered at the wounded beast. It was still alive, writhing on the ground, but showed no signs of getting up for now. Thousands of bugs spilled from its bleeding torso. Some of them were nearly at Aaron's shoes. They left oily green trails behind them.

Aaron pointed ahead. "The alleyway. We can try and make it to the edge of the village and see what's happening with the army. If things look bad, we can escape into the hills."

Cameron waved an arm and got everyone moving. "Go."

They reformed a tight group, still armed with enough bleach to make them dangerous. Several greens got in the way, but they were too slow, talons dangling uselessly at their sides until they were right up close. By then, someone would have already flicked bleach at them. Even the smallest amount of the chemical killed them.

The group funnelled into the alleyway, but it wasn't empty, and Cameron had to dispatch a pair of greens right inside the entrance. One of them was so badly infected that no human flesh remained visible. It was an elongated mass of green fur and blackened chitin, but it died like all the others.

Helen took out a nearby third with her bloody machete, which she must have retrieved from Dale's corpse. Something about that sent a chill down Aaron's spine.

With the way ahead clear, everyone picked up the pace.

A large shape lay at the opposite end of the alleyway. It was starting to get dark, the grey twilight barely enough to see by, so it wasn't until they got closer that Aaron made out what was blocking the exit. "Bodies."

Cameron saw it too. "A pile of dead greens."

Rifle fire clattered. Another body flopped backwards onto the pile.

"It's the army," said Cameron. "They're kicking arse."

"Too little too late," said Helen. "Cowards shoulda done something days ago."

"I still smell petrol," said Tom. "It's getting stronger."

Fiona shielded her eyes. "Oh shit!"

A sudden *whooshing* sound erupted, and the pile of bodies burst into flames. A hot wind blew down the alleyway. Aaron's grimy brown hair fluttered on the breeze.

"Go back the other way," said Cameron. "Move it."

"We can't," shouted Ed, clutching at his floppy blonde hair. "We're trapped."

A group of greens had entered the alleyway behind them, pressed shoulder to shoulder – a wall of deadly talons whipping in front of them.

"This goddamn alleyway," said Cameron.

Tom chuckled. "We really should learn our lesson."

"Chloe's house," said Aaron. "We can go through and make it back onto the road."

"Good idea," said Cameron. "Gold star, lad."

Everyone sprinted for the battered gate that led to Chloe's garden. They hurried through and gathered on the tiny patio. Aaron remembered Chloe had left the key in the door, but for a moment he panicked as his mind conjured images of it being gone. His fears were unfounded and he spotted the key dangling in the door handle right where Chloe had left it.

Before she died.

I can't take much more of this.

Aaron stepped over the dead green from their previous visit and unlocked the door. He shouldered it open and stepped back, wary of being attacked. Sure enough, another green appeared in the doorway.

Tom hopped in the way and flicked bleach in its face. It was dead five seconds later, crumpled inside the doorway. Cameron kicked its corpse out of the way and turned back to the others. "Keep close and watch out for each other."

The stench of burning bodies grew thick. Aaron was glad to step inside Chloe's house where the air was a little cleaner, but he became dismayed when he realised it smelled of her. His crush on her had been stupid – he knew it – but lesbian or not, he had been attracted to her. She had been pretty and sexy, without having to make a massive effort like some girls. She hadn't been trying to get noticed.

But I noticed her anyway.

And now she's gone.

Cameron stomped through the house, seeking out greens with his large bottle of bleach. The house was empty despite the living room window having been smashed. Cameron moved for the front door.

"Wait," said Tom. "The army could be right outside. What if they decide to shoot at us?"

"What choice do we have?" said Aaron. He didn't have any bleach, so he grabbed a heavy-looking lamp from a side unit. He removed the lampshade and held it like a club, but then decided it made a stupid weapon and tossed it down on the sofa with a sigh. Part of him didn't even want to fight back. He just wanted it all to be over. "If we stay here, the greens will find us. If they don't, we'll burn to death. The army is going to torch the entire village."

"I still don't know why now," said Tom. "What brought their timetable forward? Holloway said he was going to burn the village in the morning."

"I imagine we'll find out the answers soon enough," said Fiona. She weighed up a bottle of bleach in her hand. It seemed mostly empty. "Open the door, Cameron."

Cameron took the order and yanked open the door. Nothing came to attack him, so he stepped outside. Fiona and Tom went next, followed by Aaron and Helen. Then the others.

The world was ablaze.

A dozen cottages burned, thatched roofs consumed by flames. The stone walls gave some relief, and merely blackened instead of burnt, but the wooden window frames, floors, and roof timbers were all burning ferociously. Several dead greens lay in the area, many of their corpses smouldering away. In many places, the ground itself seemed to smoke.

The fungus. It's all burning. It's spreading the fire.

Good.

"The entire village is burning," said Tom. "How do we escape?"

A sudden explosion erupted somewhere behind Chloe's house. The noise made a nearby green shudder.

The army were entering the village from all over, rifles clacking endlessly.

Cameron got moving, his limp barely detectable. The others followed. Fires cropped up everywhere. The only safe destination was deeper into the village, but that would be a death sentence all of its own.

Every option we have is a bad one.

"The fire is spreading too fast," said Fiona, shielding her eyes as the air began to fill with ashes.

"Old houses," said Cameron. "We need to keep moving. We'll find a way through."

And they did. Cameron kicked in a side-access gate that led everyone into a muddy patch of garden behind one of the cottages. Part of its fencing had fallen down revealing the road beyond. It was clear.

Everyone ran.

They all hoped the road would lead them out of the village.

But it led them right to the army.

THE SOLDIERS HELD A MASSIVE HOSE. At first, it looked like they were trying to put out the fires, but the liquid coming out the end was too dirty to be water. Also, the pressure was low and the substance came out in a lethargic *glug-glug-glug*. Then it all made sense. Somehow, the army was siphoning fuel from the petrol station. It was spreading out all over the road. Holloway had found a way of burning Choirikell to the ground.

A soldier spotted Cameron and the others.

Fiona waved an arm in the air. "We need help."

The soldier dropped to a knee and fired his rifle. Through some miracle, his shot missed, but it caused everyone to scatter.

"Stay together," Cameron shouted, but it was no use. Everyone bolted in a dozen directions, desperate to avoid being shot. Only Fiona, Cameron, Aaron, Helen, and Tom stayed together near the cottage. They'd been through too much together to split up. Ed started to run but then turned around and came back. Perhaps he thought his odds were better staying.

"Back into the garden," Cameron shouted, and they ducked back through the broken fence panel. Fiona dawdled, waving both hands in the air and still shouting at the soldiers. "We're not infected. Please, just—"

Another shot rang out, splintering the fence behind her. Aaron turned back to grab her. The soldiers across the road placed a dozen shots in the backs of the fleeing survivors. A couple managed to escape into the village; five fell down dead.

Aaron yanked Fiona back into cover. "They're fucking slaughtering everyone," she said.

"They're trying to contain the fungus," Tom reasoned. "They can't risk anyone coming out and bringing it with them."

Cameron sneered. "Yoo saying they're doin' the right thing, Poshie?"

"Heaven's no. They're fucking murderers whatever the circumstances, but it doesn't change the fact that we have no safe place to go."

"We need to make a run for it," said Ed. "Make for the hills. Dale said he's a cabin somewhere out there."

Helen looked at him. "Do ye have any idea where?"

Ed shook his head. "Nah, dinnae, yoo? I mean, Dale used to be ye—"

Helen cut him off angrily. "We used to shag, Ed, that's all. I barely spent a day with him ootside of his pub."

"I know where it is," said Cameron. "It's where Dale used to take the lads shooting. Ye reckon it'll be safe there?"

Helen shrugged. "Maybe. Maybe not."

Aaron shook his head. "The fungus isn't going to stop spreading. If we have any chance of surviving, we need to head south where there are still people trying to fight it."

"He's right," said Fiona. "It's too dangerous to try and make it on our own."

More rifle fire clattered.

Ed flinched. "I say the alternative is worse. Ye really want to trust the army and the government to keep us safe?"

Aaron chewed at his lip. He didn't know what else to say. He almost didn't care.

Cameron's brow furrowed as he seemed to think. "Little English is right," he eventually said. "We need to head south. The only way to beat this thing is with manpower, and there's nae left around here."

"What if we can make it to Holloway?" asked Fiona. "What if we show him we're not infected?"

"He'll probably shoot us anyway," said Tom. "He was starting to crack up if you ask me."

"Then we're screwed whatever we do. If men like Holloway are killing innocent people, what chance do any of us have? We might as well give up."

Aaron sighed. "Maybe only one of us needs to take a risk. I could make it back to the camp and ask Holloway for mercy."

Ed nodded. "They'll nae shoot a kid, right?"

"No way," said Fiona. "Aaron isn't doing that."

"I'll go," said Helen. "I'm a woman. That might make him less likely to shoot me, but even if I'm wrong, I can't say I'd care. Either way, ye'll know one way or another if it's safe to go back to camp."

Aaron shook his head, but Cameron spoke over his concerns. "Don't get shot for the sake of it, Helen-lass." He pulled out his pistol and tried to hand it to her. "Take this."

She shrugged. "I don't need it. Just get me to this Holloway so I can speak to him. Whatever happens next is a roll of the dice."

Cameron blew out his cheeks. "It's getting dark, and it's barely possible to see through all this ash. We can creep our way through the village and find a way oot, I reckon. The army nae has enough men to cover every corner of Choirikell. They're relying on the fire to take on a life of its own and do the job for them."

Tom nodded. "Let's wait a few minutes and let the ash get thicker. Then we should make a break for it."

Everyone agreed. They took a breather, huddled in the muddy garden and keeping watch through the gaps in the fence. Meanwhile, the soldiers continued dousing the village in petrol, igniting it with thrown candles and zippo lighters. The flames were starting to creep towards the garden, but that would work in their favour. It would provide a screen between them and the soldiers. They could make a mad dash across the village, moving deeper into Choirikell before looping around and making it onto the main road south. Failing that, they could just carry on running into the hills, hoping not to freeze or starve to death before the fungus reached them. Fiona and Cameron still had bleach, but it was barely enough to take down a half-dozen greens.

After five minutes, they could wait no longer. The flames had got close enough that they were all sweating. It was the first time Aaron had been truly warm since arriving in the Highlands, and after being cold for so long, the heat was almost unbearable.

"Okay," said Cameron. "Ye see Barry's bakery over there? There's a path that leads right through an archway beside it. The main road from the church is on the other side. If it's clear, we can head doon the hill and get to the edge of the camp."

Aaron nodded. "I remember it. The beast chased me there."

"Aye. Well, let's hope for the same luck ye had then. Okay, everyone, move!"

The group broke cover and ran with their heads down. As they had hoped, the fire created a screen between them and the soldiers with the hose, so the soldiers did not see them. Rather than heading deeper into Choirikell, the soldiers seemed to be moving laterally, cutting through the village from one side to the other. It made sense in a way. They were trying to create a wall of fire to stop the fungus spreading south. Hopefully, the fire would spread to eventually consume the entire village. It was a good use of the limited petrol they had. The roads shone with it, trails of fire spreading in every direction.

Cameron was as quick as a bull despite the bullet lodged in his backside, and he no longer showed any effects of being drunk earlier in the day. Everyone else hurried a few paces behind him, and they all managed to make it to the bakery without being shot. Aaron spotted the scattered bodies of the people from the pub who had tried to run. He hadn't even learned their names.

We came to rescue these people, but all we ended up doing was trading Ryan, Miles, and Chloe for Helen and Ed. I wish I could take it back.

I want my brother back.

The group moved through a covered pathway beside the bakery, a gap between buildings, and reached the road on the other side. It was thick with greens in the direction of the church and the army was approaching from the direction of the camp.

"Shite," said Cameron. "Can we not get one wee break?"

"The greens or the army," said Tom. "Take your pick."

"Looks like I'm nae gunna make it to camp," said Helen. "So here's plan B."

Before anyone could stop her, Helen broke from cover and rushed out into the road. She approached the soldiers, both hands above her head. Once they spotted her, they raised their rifles. "Please," she shouted. "I'm nae infected. I've been hiding oot alone, but ye set fire to ma home."

The soldiers began to yell back at her, but they didn't fire. Unlike the soldiers with the hose, these men were not setting fires. Clearly, they were a clean-up crew, covering the gaps where the fire had yet to reach.

But they're not shooting, thought Aaron. *That's a good sign.*

One of the shouting voices overrode the others, ordering

Helen to her knees. She did as she was told, hands remaining above her head. Looking at her from behind, Aaron realised what a poor state Helen was in. Darkened bloodstains covered the back of her blouse, and her hair was a dirty, knotted mess. Aaron looked at his other companions and saw exhaustion on their soot-blackened faces. They were all close to breaking. This was their last hope. They couldn't do this on their own much longer.

I can't do it without you, Ryan.

"I'm okay," Helen told the soldiers. "I'll strip naked if ye want and ye can check me over."

A couple of the soldiers exchanged glances. The situation was too dire for laughter, but one of them appeared to smirk. They were close enough now that it would be impossible for Cameron to get everyone out of there without being seen. The fire at their back made it impossible to head back the way they had come. If Helen failed, they were doomed.

"We need to shoot her," said one of the men.

"Aye, we have orders," said another. "No exceptions."

The soldier who had spoken loudest stepped away from the others. It was a woman, and she looked at Helen with suspicion. "And what if I check ye over and find something I nae like?"

"Then I suppose ye'll have to kill me."

"What's yer name?"

"Helen."

"All right, Helen. I suppose you better come with us. Lieutenant Holloway can decide what to do with ye."

Aaron glanced at Cameron. "It's working. They're not going to shoot her."

"Feck this. We have orders," said one of the soldiers.

"Stand down, Dan."

Cameron glared. "It's that bastard again. He's a pain in ma feckin' backside, literally."

Still wearing his black beanie hat, the private stepped forward and continued to argue. "Holloway gave us orders to shoot anyone trying to get oot the village."

"I'm using my discretion, private. This woman seems unin-fected to me, and it'll be easy enough to verify back at camp."

Beanie Hat strolled towards Helen, his rifle raised, and pointed at her. "Sorry, Sarge, but that's fecking bullshit and you know it."

"Stand doon, Private! Stand doon!"

But Beanie Hat continued to ignore her. He sighted down his rifle, preparing to take a shot. "Ye can shoot me in the back, Sarge, or ye can do ye job and follow orders. This bitch is dead either way. There's nae other choice."

Cameron leapt out of the alleyway, whipping out his pistol and pointing it at Beanie Hat's head. The private was taken by surprise and immediately swung his rifle around. Rather than try to dodge out of the way, Cameron strode towards the man, pistol aimed right at his forehead. It created a standoff. "I'd say there's plenty of choices, pal. One choice is that I shoot ye right in yer feckin mug."

"Yer'll nae get the chance," said Beanie Hat, eyes narrowing behind his scope. "Ye'll be dead before ye hit the ground."

Aaron leapt out of cover, hands above his head. "Please stop. We aren't infected. We just need help."

The sergeant flinched in recognition. "Yer the civilians from quarantine?"

Aaron realised it was the medic who had tended to their wounds after Dr Gerard's disappearance. "Yeah. It's us. We went back into the village to warn some other survivors in the pub. They needed to know about the fires. It was the right thing to do."

Tom stepped out of cover next. It left Ed and Fiona with little choice but to do the same. "We were supposed to have until morning," he said. "What happened?" He looked back at the approaching greens. There were several dozen of them, now only thirty metres away. "Although I can imagine."

Beanie Hat growled. "This is getting ridiculous. Sarge, we need to take these people doon. They could all be infected."

"We're not," said Helen, "and like I said, we're happy to strip doon. Why would you shoot innocent people when there's a choice not to?"

The sergeant nodded. "I agree. No one's getting shot here. We'll examine ye all back at camp, and we'll have to make it fast because those things are coming for us. I need to bring backup."

Helen nodded. "Thank you."

"Not this one," said Beanie Hat, continuing to glare down his rifle at Cameron. "Him and me have unfinished business."

"Aye," said Cameron, pistol still pointed at his face. "Ye mean like when ye shot me in the arse like a coward?"

"Just a doon payment, and I'm ready to pay the balance."

"Stand doon, Dan," the sergeant ordered. Two soldiers stood with her, but they didn't seem to know where to aim their rifles.

"I'm nae gunna do that, Sarge. In fact, I say it's yoo what needs to stand doon. Mikey, Jimbo, you need to make a decision. Do ye want to risk everything by letting these people into camp, or do you want to follow orders like me? The entire feckin' country is depending on us doing our jobs."

"We're not infected," said Helen. Her hands were still above her head despite no one aiming a weapon at her.

"Stand doon," the sergeant said again. "We don't have time for this. Yer gonna get us all killed."

The greens were getting closer.

"Time to choose," said Beanie Hat. "Mikey, Jimbo?"

One the two soldiers raised their rifle and aimed it at the sergeant. The shock on the woman's face almost knocked her down. She turned to the mutinous man in outrage, but kept her rifle lowered. "Mikey, what the hell do ye think yer doing?"

"Dan's right, Sarge. We can't take the risk. These civilians already disobeyed orders once when they left camp. We can't let them live after being exposed out here."

"They're not soldiers, Mikey. They're civilians. If we're not protecting them, then what the hell we even doing oot here?"

"Surviving," said Beanie Hat.

"Ye take that shot, Dan, and ye'll be dead a second later, I warn ye."

"Stand down, Sarge," said Mikey. "I dinnae want to shoot ye."

The sergeant glared at him. "Yoo better, because yer feckin' done for if ye don't."

"Shoot her, Mikey," said Beanie Hat. "We've gone too far now not to."

Mikey suddenly seemed unsure. He kept the rifle on the sergeant, but he didn't pull the trigger. "I... We... It doesn't need to go that way."

"Bullshit," said Beanie Hat.

The sergeant sneered. "Do yer own dirty work, Private. Or aren't yer man enough?"

"Oh, I'm man enough, you stupid bitch." Beanie Hat whipped around and aimed his rifle at the sergeant, "and I fancy a promotion."

Cameron pulled the trigger and blew Beanie Hat's brains out. "Eejit!"

"Yer a dead man." Mikey immediately changed his aim to Cameron, sighting down the rifle and—

The sergeant lifted her rifle and shot her own man in the chest. He flew back like a train had hit him, ending up on his back in the centre of the road.

The remaining man – Jimbo – put both hands in the air, rifle hanging from his neck by its strap. "Hey, I'm with you, Sarge. I don't want to kill civilians any more than you do."

The sergeant turned around and glared at Cameron. "Ye shouldna done that."

"He was gunna shoot ye, lass. Ye should be thanking me."

The sergeant looked back at Mikey's body, and then at Beanie Hat's. She put a hand to her face and groaned. "Christ, this is fucked up."

"No, it's all fine," said Tom. He stepped out from behind Cameron, palms open and on display. "The greens are about to reach us, and we need to move, but as far as anyone needs to know, your men died fighting them. The situation may have turned bad, but you were trying to do the right thing. If we have any chance of getting through this, then we need people like you to keep doing what's right. Otherwise, we're fighting a war that's already lost."

The sergeant sighed. She looked back at Jimbo, who shrugged his shoulders to show that he was on board with whatever direction she took. Instead of speaking, she lifted her rifle and aimed it at Cameron. Cameron ducked just in time to avoid a bullet to the face. Behind him, a green fell down dead. A dozen more were right behind it.

"I say we get oot of here and work oot the rest later."

Cameron spun around and fired off a shot from his pistol. The bullet struck an infected woman in the throat and caused her to make a whistling sound. His next shot obliterated her mushy head.

Jimbo and the sergeant opened fire, taking down six greens in a matter of seconds. Back to business, the sergeant grabbed Aaron by the shoulder and threw him into the middle of the road. "Get moving, people. We're going to need backup."

9

The sergeant and Jimbo walked backwards, taking careful shots that took down the approaching greens one by one. There must have been nearly thirty of them in total, and they were coming faster than they were falling. Eventually, the soldiers would have no choice but to turn tail and run. Cameron had already tucked his pistol back into his waistband and was now shoving Aaron along with him. Ed, Fiona, Helen and Tom were right behind. They weren't out of the woods yet, but they weren't dead either.

As expected, the sergeant was forced to call a retreat, so everyone began to run along the centre of the road. It was rain slick but free from fungus. Nearby, the village burned bright against the night sky. It reminded Aaron of bonfire night. He tried to count how many he'd been to with Ryan and realised there were more than he could even remember. They began with him being small, sitting on his big brother's shoulders so that he could see the fireworks more easily, and they ended last year, when Aaron had been sullen and moody, wanting to go home and play video games.

Fireworks are boring. I remember saying it.

I remember the look on Ryan's face. He thought he'd lost me. Lost his kid brother.

But really I lost him.

It didn't take long to make it back to the army camp. The floodlights were lit and the single bonfire still burned. Things were different though. Soldiers were firing their rifles amongst the tents. People were shouting. There was chaos everywhere.

"Damn it," said the sergeant. "Things are still bad."

"What happened?" Tom demanded.

The soldier looked back at the pursuing greens. They had a few seconds to rest, but no more than a minute. "A buzzard came into camp – a big fat thing the size of a house cat. It wouldn't shoo away, so one of the men shot it. It came apart like an egg, and those bugs spilled out everywhere. Next thing we know, there are more birds swooping doon on our heids. At the same time, a bunch of feckin' Kermits come at our perimeter. It was a goddamn coordinated attack. Holloway had to bring our plans forward. This place needs to burn."

Everyone looked at one another. They had been fearing it for a while, but now it was certain that the enemy was capable of planning attacks. Things were hopeless.

The sergeant reached a hand out to the other man's arm. "Jimbo, I need to get these civilians to Holloway. Go get whoever you can find and take care of those greens coming doon the road."

Jimbo nodded and took off, while the sergeant sprinted towards camp, prompting everyone else to follow. They passed by the male quarantine tent, and Ryan shuddered when he saw its earlier safety in tatters. Dark splotches covered the canvas walls, and there was a gaping tear on one side. The picnic table outside had been upended. A rat scuttled out from behind it. Cameron booted it like a football and it went hurtling into the air.

Ahead, four soldiers stood in a huddle, firing at a small group of greens that were coming out of the hills. One of the men was

Corporal Kay. When he saw them, he was staggered. "Yoo feckers are still breathing?"

Aaron shook his head. "Not all of us."

It took a moment, but the corporal understood what Aaron was telling him. "Ah, shite. I'm sorry, lad."

Aaron nodded.

"The vicar too?"

"Aye," said Cameron. "I know ye said ye'd shoot us if we came back, but it looks like ye could use a hand."

Kay took a shot at a green, then sighed. "I'm in nae mood to see any more men die tonight, so I suggest ye go see Holloway and beg fer yer lives. Hey, Sarge, where's Dan and the others? I could use some more men."

"Jimbo's dealing with another problem. Dan and Mikey are dead."

Kay winced, and his eyes slowly settled on Cameron. "Is that right, aye?"

Cameron nodded. "Sorry for yer loss."

"Yeah, well, right, I suppose there'll be time to mourn him later, eh? Ye best get going."

"Holloway," said the sergeant. "Where is he?"

"Losing his shit inside the command tent. Tread carefully."

The sergeant nodded in thanks and then took off. Aaron and the others chased after her. They quickly reached the command tent, but before they had a chance to go inside, Holloway came spilling out. His shirt was completely unbuttoned, showing a vest underneath. He was sweating and his hair was a mess. The look in his eyes was manic. When he saw the sergeant and the others, he almost seemed to doubt his own eyes. "What are you people doing back here? Have you not caused enough trouble? I'll have you all shot. Shot, do you hear me?"

"We're not here to cause trouble," said Cameron. "We're here to help. We found survivors at the pub, but your men gunned 'em all doon. If they had nae done that, ye would have had another dozen bodies to help ye fight. We're what's left, so respectfully, we ask ye to use yer heid and let us live. We're nae infected, and we know how to fight these things."

"Bleach," said Tom. "We used it in the village. It's their kryptonite."

Holloway nodded. "Gerard said as much might be true before the coward ran for the hills. We have some in the infirmary, and it'll be easy enough to find in the field. Thank you for the intel. I just wish it were not too late."

"Why is it too late?" asked Fiona. "The fire is working. We just need to pull everyone back to the camp so we can leave."

Holloway sighed. "I'll put up a flare, but the camp is overrun. We can't turn our backs with the enemy everywhere like this."

"Noise," said Aaron. "The greens can't stand loud noises. It stuns them. We're starting to learn their weaknesses. Bleach, fire, noise. We have a chance here."

The sergeant nodded. "What do ye want us to do, sir?"

Holloway was a ghost, his mind in a faraway place. He swallowed a lump in his throat and spoke in a weak voice. "Do whatever you can, and pray that it's enough."

The officer wandered off back into his tent.

"Well," said Helen, "that's the scary officer you were telling me aboot, eh?"

"He's seen better days," said Aaron.

Cameron shrugged. "At least he didnae shoot us."

"Come on," said the sergeant. "Get the bleach from the infirmary if ye think it'll help. I'm gunna go help where I can. Yoo do the same."

Cameron saluted. "Aye. What's ye name, lass?"

"Brenda, but never call me that. People around here call me Boon."

"Thanks, Boon."

"Try not to die." She took off into the camp.

Tom started towards the nearby infirmary tent. "Guess it's time to arm up?"

"We could always run," said Helen. "Nothing to stop us hitting the road right now and getting oot of here."

"Not so long ago," said Cameron, "I might have done just that, but not now. I've nae time for fascists, but there are good men and women in this camp. We should help 'em."

"I agree," said Tom. "Surprisingly."

"We all do," said Fiona.

Helen gave Aaron a nudge. "If things get any uglier, I'm dragging ye arse home to ye mamma."

Aaron chuckled. "Fair enough."

Ed was clutching at himself nervously. "I know I'm new around here, but I'd really like not to die. Can we do what we're going to do before I shit my keks and run fer the hills?"

Aaron went and patted the lad on the back. "Welcome to our happy little family."

THEY WERE DISMAYED by the amount of bleach they found inside the infirmary tent. Only two bottles, three litres in each. Cameron took one and Helen the other. It left the rest of them unarmed, but there was no point in arguing over it.

They headed back outside the infirmary to greet the same chaos they had left behind. Several groups of soldiers were firing their rifles wildly, aiming at fluttering black shadows or the greens approaching from the hills. The nearby landscape was dotted with shadows, all of them getting closer.

Car horns began to blare.

Aaron looked towards the rear of the camp, to where the old trucks were all lined up. There, Holloway was directing a group of soldiers to blare the horns.

"He listened to us," said Fiona. "He's managed to get his shit together."

"Just in time," said Tom.

All around the camp, the greens started to convulse – but only intermittently.

"It's not high-pitched enough," said Aaron, realising it wasn't working. "The sound isn't hurting them enough."

"Well, it's better than nowt," said Cameron. "It's slowing 'em doon at least."

"Hey," said Fiona, "I have an idea."

Everyone watched her hurry through camp. They ran after her, lucky not to get pounced on by the enemy. Fiona eventually stopped beside the camp's bell.

Aaron understood immediately and gave a grim smile. "Dinner's ready."

Fiona grabbed the handle and started ringing the bell. Its pitch was only an octave or two higher than the car horns, but its hollow din instantly hurt their ears. It hurt the greens even more.

A fat buzzard fell out of the sky, allowing a pair of soldiers to come out of cover and put a bullet in it. Further away, a group of greens began to convulse, making them sitting ducks for Corporal Kay and his men. They took down the stunned creatures and then rushed off to help elsewhere.

Ed whistled. "I'll be damned."

"It's working," said Aaron. "The greens can't attack."

"But we still can," said Cameron, lifting his bottle of bleach. "Come on, let's have some fun."

Helen and Cameron led the way with their bleach. They encountered more fallen buzzards, and these were dispatched with the merest of dribbles. Then they encountered an infected man with a huge round gut poking out from beneath a fungus-covered jumper.

"It's old Andrew Lennon, the milkman." Cameron chuckled. "Scouse accent so thick even Stevie Gerard wouldn't have understood him."

"He was from Runcorn," said Helen, and then shrugged. "We dated a few times."

Cameron sighed. "Yer'll never walk alone, brother." He

doused the green in bleach and left it to squeal and squirm. They didn't wait for it to die. There was still too much to do.

The soldiers were regaining control over the camp. Without the threat of whipping talons and swooping buzzards, they were able to come out of cover and methodically dispatch the enemy. Fiona continued striking the bell while Holloway had his men keep on the truck horns. Up the hill, Choirikell was an inferno, the fire having taken on a life of its own. They had scorched the earth. Nothing left to do now except clean up and get out.

Boon saw them standing in camp and came on over. She was smiling. "You knew to ring the bell?"

Aaron nodded. "We've used sound against them before. Anything high-pitched sends them into a fit."

"It can't be that easy."

Cameron shrugged. "About time we had a break, do ye nae think?"

"I suppose yer right. Well, I'm extra glad I didn't execute yoo folks back in the village now."

"Yeah," said Tom. "Us too." He looked back towards the bell. "I'll go and relieve Fiona before her shoulders give oot." He shook his head. "Christ, I'm turning Scottish."

Aaron stood, realising he no longer had to fight for his life – at least not right at that moment. Suddenly, he had time to think, to notice his heart beating in his chest, to feel the aches all over his body. He fell to the mud, breathless.

Boon was right down next to him. "What is it? What's wrong?"

Aaron couldn't speak. Couldn't catch his breath.

"Are you having an asthma attack?"

Aaron shook his head.

"Can you try and breathe slowly?"

Aaron shook his head.

Cameron knelt beside him, putting a large hand on his back and rubbing. "Lad's lost his brother, and he doesnae know what to do next."

Aaron nodded.

Cameron pulled him into a hug. "I wish I could tell ye everything would be okay, lad, but I doubt it will be. All I can say is that ye have friends. Friends who are going to make sure you get home to ye ma. Never thought I'd said it, but ye can rely on me. Huh, Miles would be proud."

Aaron managed to speak. "B-But wh-what if my mam's dead?"

"Yer thinking too far ahead, lad. Tell ye the truth, not thinking ahead has always been ma problem, but right now it'll nae do ye any favours. Focus on putting one foot in front of the other and nae further, ye hear?"

Aaron managed to reconnect with his breathing. He focused on relaxing and slowing down his inhalations. Eventually, he was taking in air normally. Cameron let go of him and bumped their foreheads together. Then he stood up.

Aaron remained on the ground for another minute.

Cheering sounded in the distance.

Soldiers started coming down the hill from Choirikell, returning back to camp. By now, all of the greens in camp had been dispatched. The floodlights illuminated their corpses. Dead buzzards littered the ground. The war was far from over, but they had won tonight's battle. It was a victory sorely needed.

Holloway appeared in the centre of camp and yelled into a megaphone. "Grab whatever you can and load up the trucks. Honour our dead. We're leaving this godforsaken hill in thirty minutes."

The tired soldiers in camp obeyed with excitement. The thought of getting off this drab, death-covered hill was probably as enticing to them as it was to Aaron and his friends. It was time to go and never look back.

Aaron got to his feet while Fiona and Tom came over from the bell. They shared hugs with one another and pats on the back. Even Helen. Then they stood and watched Choirikell burn in the distance.

"Had some good memories here," said Cameron.

Helen nodded. "Bad ones too."

"Aye, plenty of those."

"I'm sorry," said Aaron. "This place was your home."

Cameron shrugged. "One place is as good as another. Long as there's a decent boozer and good company."

Soldiers continued to flood down the hill from the burning village. Some were injured, limping and holding on to one another. If any of them were infected, Holloway would likely put a bullet in them, and the horrific part was that it would be the right thing to do. This wasn't the flu they were dealing with. If the fungus got inside you, you were already dead.

"Looks like plenty made it," said Tom.

"Aye," said Ed. "Wish there were more though."

"Time to find out what's left elsewhere," said Fiona.

Somewhere far off in the distance was a scream. It was so brief and unexpected that Aaron thought he'd imagined it. But then he heard another.

More screams began to break out from the edge of the village.

Tom groaned. "What's happening?"

"Nowt good," said Cameron.

Boon raised her rifle, but she clearly didn't know where to aim. "Something's coming."

Aaron nodded. The next battle was about to begin, and he had a good idea who it would be against.

Along came the beast.

THE BEAST APPEARED at the top of the hill, blocking the glow from the burning village. It was so big, it was like watching a whale grow legs and walk the Earth. It still resembled some kind of bizarre, giant squid, its flesh shimmering in the moonlight, but it was now much wider. It enveloped the land like a giant mollusc, slithering over sprinting soldiers and making them disappear. It was a sponge, soaking up anything alive that stood in its way.

The remaining soldiers fired their weapons. A few even

tossed grenades. The assault obliterated the beast's flesh but did nothing to stop its advance. It continued, relentlessly, to slither down the hill, taking more and more soldiers into its bulk. Flesh and chitin shed in chunks as more bullets hit it, but it was like scratching the skin off a sunburn. Nothing went deep enough to do the behemoth any harm.

Fiona raced back over to the camp bell and started ringing it. Over and over again.

It had no effect on the beast.

Several soldiers turned and ran. Others tried to hold their ground. Within moments they were hoovered up by the beast's slithering mass. It moved deceptively quickly, a speeding, gelatinous hovercraft.

Holloway barked orders, but they mostly consisted of telling everyone to shoot the damn thing. It was a doomed strategy and most of his men panicked and ran.

The beast reached the edge of camp, crashing through the male quarantine tent and hoovering up soldiers left and right. Corporal Kay stood in its path, firing from a shotgun. A tendril whipped out from behind the beast and sliced his head clean off. It rolled through the mud like a football.

Cameron swore, then raced towards the beast before anyone could stop him.

Tom grabbed Aaron and pulled him backwards. "Time to go. We can't fight this thing."

"He's right," said Helen. "Ye stay here, ye die."

Aaron struggled away from them. "But Cameron!"

"He's a big boy," said Fiona. "We have to get out of here, Aaron."

Aaron nodded, realising that the only thing left in camp was a certain death. Somehow, despite the pain in his chest, he wanted to live. "The trucks. We need to get one of the trucks."

"RETREAT!" Holloway shouted, finally seeing sense. The officer was firing a rifle, but he threw it down at his feet as he realised it was no more dangerous than a broom handle. He started grabbing men all around him and pulling them back, yelling in their faces to run for their lives. Everyone had the same idea as Aaron and headed for the trucks. Engines began to rumble.

"If we don't move," said Tom, "we're going to get left behind."

The beast slithered across camp, sucking up the bodies of the dead – green and human alike. Men and women screamed as tendrils whipped at them, or they were crushed beneath its massive bulk.

Boon fired her rifle nearby.

Cameron got within ten metres of the beast and stopped, hurling his bottle of bleach overhead and managing to arc it right into the beast's path. It hoovered up the bottle and carried on.

But then it stopped.

The beast's massive bulk flattened and spread out. It began to shake. It bellowed in agony as black smoke began to rise up from some kind of open orifice on its back, a hole like that of a whale.

Cameron ran back to the others, grinning all the way. "I got the fecker!"

"Ye did," said Boon, lowering her rifle. "Yer a goddamn madman."

"Aye, I am that."

The beast continued to tremble and shake, bellow and thrash, but slowly it rose back up, its width narrowing and its height increasing. It whipped out a bunch of tendrils and caught a nearby group of soldiers still standing and fighting. They fell to the ground, bleeding from torn-open flesh.

"Damn it," said Tom. "It's still coming."

"It doesnae die," said Ed, shaking his head in horror.

"Back to plan A, then," said Helen. "Get to the trucks."

They turned and raced for the rear of the camp where the trucks were parked in a line. A dozen had already departed, screeching off into the distance. Only four remained. Helen and the others headed for the nearest, but another man was already inside the cabin and about to close the door.

Cameron caught up and grabbed the man by the wrist in time to stop him driving off. "We need a lift, pal. Can we get in the back? If ye dinnae— Oh shite!"

Aaron saw the way Cameron was staring up at the driver and didn't like it. "What's wrong?"

Cameron gave the driver a hefty yank, pulling him out of the cab by his wrist. The man landed awkwardly and slipped in the mud. When he got up, he was trembling and panicking. It was easy to see why.

"You're infected," said Fiona.

"*Really* infected," said Ed.

The soldier shook his head. "I'm fine. I'm fine."

But the man was not fine. He had a thick gash across his face, all the way from his hairline to his jaw. Already it was oozing green oil. There was no way to help him. They had tried it with Chloe. He was a dead man.

"Ye need to stay behind," said Cameron. "Sorry, pal, but yer done for."

"No. No, I just need to get to a hospital. I just..." He put a hand out to Cameron and tried to grab him.

Cameron dodged backwards out of reach. "Listen, pal, ye—"

A gunshot rang out, close enough to cause everyone to duck and cover their ears.

The driver froze like a statue, a red dot growing on his forehead. The back of his head had sprayed across the outside of the truck door. His body flopped face down in the mud. Boon stepped over him, her rifle emitting a thin trail of grey smoke from its barrel. "Dinnae worry. This guy was always a right prick."

Cameron chuckled, a little nervously. "Aye."

Everyone clambered into the back of the truck while Aaron sat up front with Boon. The keys were in the ignition so she started the engine.

The beast slithered quickly towards them, obliterating the remainder of the camp. The sole bonfire continued to blaze behind it, making it appear like a demon from the depths of hell, shrouded by flames.

Boon punched the steering wheel. "We'll never make it in time. This thing is too fast."

"Try," said Aaron.

Boon nodded and put the truck in reverse. She loosed the handbrake and the heavy vehicle lurched backwards.

Helen was standing alone outside, right in the beam of the headlights.

"Shit!" said Aaron. "Stop!"

Boon slammed on the brakes and swore. "What the hell is she doing?"

Helen raced towards another of the parked trucks. Only two others remained, but there was no one left trying to get inside them. The beast made a beeline for the vehicles and was only halted when Holloway appeared in its way. The officer wielded a pair of handguns, which he fired off one after the other, more like a gangster than a soldier. There was a crazed look on his face. He showed no fear, only madness.

"He's insane." Boon blasted the truck's horn. "Get the hell outta there, man!"

The beast rose up, its mass a giant tidal wave that came crashing down on top of Holloway.

And that was it.

He was gone.

Another engine grumbled to life.

Aaron leant over Boon's lap and saw that Helen had got inside another truck and started it. She was gripping the steering wheel, staring ahead. Aaron had no idea what she was doing.

Helen's truck shot forward. Instead of turning to exit the camp, she steered right towards the beast.

The beast no longer had a face or a head, but it appeared to notice the incoming vehicle because it appeared to turn slightly, a wave of movement vibrating through its wobbling flesh.

"She's going to ram it," said Aaron. There was no way such a thing would kill the beast, so it was a reckless, stupid thing to do, but he understood it. "She's trying to buy us time."

Helen managed to get the truck up to speed before it went crashing into the beast. The front end immediately disappeared into its gelatinous mass, being absorbed like everything else, but its momentum caused the beast to fold backwards on itself, a liquid changing direction.

It flopped backwards, right into the blazing bonfire.

Immediately, the beast's flesh ignited as if it were doused in petrol. It had slithered though a village soaked in the stuff. Had it absorbed petrol into itself as it slithered through the village? The soldiers had been pouring the stuff everywhere.

Black smoke filled the air and the beast's green flesh turned black.

Cameron appeared beside Aaron's door. He had jumped out the back to see what the hold-up was and banged on the window until Aaron unwound it. "The hell is happening? We getting oot o' here or what?" Then he saw the beast burning on the bonfire and gasped. "Squeeze ma bawbag. What happened?"

"Helen. She..." Aaron shook his head and sighed.

Cameron nodded. "Aye. Always wild, that one."

There was a screech of rending metal.

The rear wheels of the truck embedded in the beast's torso began to spin. They bit at the muddy earth, trying to get a grip, and when they eventually did, the crumpled truck rocketed backwards. It came to a stop just as quickly, rocking on its springs. Its front was a twisted mess and covered in a thick green liquid, yet somehow the remnants of a door swung open. From inside the flattened cabin, a body slithered out through a tiny gap.

Helen fell to the mud, clutching her ribs and gasping. Cameron raced to gather her up. She was okay. Winded, but unhurt, she put an arm around Cameron's neck and limped towards the other truck. After a few steps, she stopped and turned back. "That was fer Miles, ye bastard piece of shit!"

"I'll get her in the back," Cameron shouted up to Aaron. "Get a rush on, will ye?"

Boon was shaking her head in disbelief. "They really built these things to last back in the day, eh?"

Aaron was laughing, utterly stunned. He watched the beast burning on the bonfire and almost felt festive. What he was seeing was vengeance. Vengeance of an angry mankind. Suddenly, his mind did what Cameron told him it must not. It thought way ahead.

Aaron pictured a thousand beasts like this one burning to death as mankind fought back. As mankind rose a fist into the air and clearly stated that *enough is enough*.

"This is our home." Aaron reached into his pocket and took out Ryan's letter. He clutched it firmly, feeling closer to his brother. "They're not going to take it from us."

Boon got the truck onto the road, and soon after they were heading south.

Behind them, Choirikell burned until there was nothing left.

EPILOGUE

Ant Man 2. *That was the last thing we did together. Just us and a half-decent movie about a tiny little Paul Rudd. It was perfect and I didn't even know it. I was too busy thinking about wedding dresses and flower arrangements, but none of that fucking shit was important. What really mattered was the small things I took for granted. Ant Man 2. Fuck, what I would do to be back at that cinema right now, holding Ryan's hand. I would sit through that movie all over again.*

Ant Man 2.

Fuck.

Sophie was done. Finished.

"I'm not hiding any more, Nancy," she said. "If we stay here any longer, we'll lose the chance to ever leave."

"You think I don't want to go find my boys? Sophie, I know you love Ryan, but killing yourself isn't going to solve anything. Just be sensible, please."

"I need to be with him. If that means I have to hike my way to Scotland, I will, but won't you come with me? We can make it out there, I know it."

"Are you soft in the head, you daft cow? I'm pushing sixty. My hiking days are behind me. Besides, I know my boys. They'll find their way home. They always do."

Sophie rolled her eyes. Ryan's mother had never been her favourite person, but right now they were all each other had. Family. That had always been the plan, but things had happened way sooner than expected. Nancy was her mother-in-law and partner in survival whether there had been a wedding or not. In fact, she was closer to her mother-in-law than ever.

All it took was the end of the world.

The supermarket they had been staying in was starting to look more like a homeless shelter. More and more bedraggled people appeared every day. Many were taken away by the police, probably to be shot and burned on a fire. Nobody was ignorant of what it meant to be infected with the fungus.

The food was nearly all gone after just one week and people were starting to steal and stockpile. Nancy might have been comforted by the presence of police officers, but there were less and less of them every day. Were they deserting? Or dying?

Manchester had been a war zone before the fungus even arrived. Once word of the infected – or invasion – had broken out, people all over the city had panicked. Rioting and looting took place on a massive scale, and Sophie had immediately gone to check on Ryan's mam, partly because she couldn't get hold of Ryan as she hoped his mother would have. But she hadn't heard a thing. The phones were all dead, and while the television switched on, there were only a couple of channels still working. Most of the news came from daily leaflets distributed by the *Manchester Evening News*, and every day the news got worse. At first, it was about a strange virus leaked from an errant meteorite. Then it was a Chinese terror attack. Then it was aliens. One flyer came out claiming the crisis was a Heaven-sent plague meant to purge the Earth of sinners. Sophie didn't care much for the reasons, she just didn't want to stay inside this ransacked supermarket any more. It was like being a spectator in her own life. She had given up control to the authorities, become a sheep.

What she wanted most was to take charge. Even if she ended up dead, she wanted to make her own decisions. She couldn't wait any longer, praying for Ryan to find her, or for the world to right itself.

I have to go to him. He's never been a proactive kind of guy. He's too chill for that. Kind of what I love about him. No, he needs me to come to him. I know it. He needs my help.

Just like he did the day we met, with that bloody goose.

That bloody goose.

"I really think we should stay here," said Nancy. "What if we leave and Aaron and Ryan turn up looking for us? We could end up missing each other."

"And what if they never make it here at all, Nancy? That would mean you never get to see your boys ever again. Are you okay with that?"

Nancy shook her head. "Of course not."

Sophie looked around at the weary faces all around. One man, a few beds over, had been eyeing her up constantly over the last few days, and there was no doubt in her mind about what he was thinking. People had already started to steal food and toilet paper. How long before they started taking other things that didn't belong to them? If not for the presence of grimy-faced children, she feared things would have already degenerated further.

"I'm leaving first thing in the morning," said Sophie. "Things are getting bad here, and I don't want to be around when the shit finally hits the fan. I don't care if you're pushing sixty, Nancy. I won't leave you here. You're coming with me, okay?"

"Oh, am I now? Young lady, let me remind you that—"

Sophie slammed a tin of peas against the ground. It echoed off the high ceilings and caught everyone's attention. It also cut Nancy off. Sophie leant in and spoke quietly. "Look here, you grumpy old bag. I am not abandoning you here, so if I have to drag you by your fat ears, I will."

Nancy tapped at her earlobes. "Fat ears?"

"You should really wear your hair down. Anyway, we're leaving, okay? We are a pair of strong-willed women and we do not take shit from anyone. Staying here like good little pets is not who we are. I know how much Ryan looks up to you, Nancy, so don't let him down now. We're going to get out of this prison and go find your sons, whatever it takes. I want my fucking wedding; do you hear me?"

Nancy glared at her for a moment, but then she smiled. "No wonder Ryan loves you. He needs a strong woman in his life."

"And he needs his mam. Are you with me?"

"No, young lady, *you* are with *me*. Now get some sleep. Scotland's a long way to walk."

Sophie lay down in her sleeping bag and hugged her pillow. "I'm coming for you, honey," she whispered to herself. "Just hold on until I get there."

Don't miss out on your FREE Iain Rob Wright horror pack. Five terrifying books sent straight to your inbox.

No strings attached & signing up is a doddle.

Just click here

PLEA FROM THE AUTHOR

Hey, Reader. So you got to the end of my book. I hope that means you enjoyed it. Whether or not you did, I would just like to thank you for giving me your valuable time to try and entertain you. I am truly blessed to have such a fulfilling job, but I only have that job because of people like you; people kind enough to give my books a chance and spend their hard-earned money buying them. For that I am eternally grateful.

If you would like to find out more about my other books then please visit my website for full details. You can find it at:

www.iainrobwright.com.

Also feel free to contact me on Facebook, Twitter, or email (all details on the website), as I would love to hear from you.

If you enjoyed this book and would like to help, then you could think about leaving a review on Amazon, Goodreads, or anywhere else that readers visit. The most important part of how well a book sells is how many positive reviews it has, so if you leave me one then you are directly helping me to continue on this journey as a full time writer. Thanks in advance to anyone who does. It means a lot.

ALSO BY IAIN ROB WRIGHT

Animal Kingdom

AZ of Horror

2389

Holes in the Ground (with J.A.Konrath)

Sam

ASBO

The Final Winter

The Housemates

Sea Sick, Ravage, Savage

The Picture Frame

Wings of Sorrow

The Gates, Legion, Extinction, Defiance, Resurgence, Rebirth

TAR

House Beneath the Bridge

The Peeling

Blood on the bar

Escape!

Dark Ride

12 Steps

The Room Upstairs

Soft Target, Hot Zone, End Play

The Spread: Book 1

The Spread: Book 2

Iain Rob Wright is one of the UK's most successful horror and suspense writers, with novels including the critically acclaimed, THE FINAL WINTER; the disturbing bestseller, ASBO; and the wicked screamfest, THE HOUSEMATES.

His work is currently being adapted for graphic novels, audio books, and foreign audiences. He is an active member of the Horror Writer Association and a massive animal lover.

www.iainrobwright.com
FEAR ON EVERY PAGE

For more information
www.iainrobwright.com
iain.robert.wright@hotmail.co.uk

Printed in Great Britain
by Amazon